Kinmara

Brackenbelly

And the
Beast of Hogg-Bottom Farm

Also Available by Gareth Baker

ROGUE RACER

◉

Time Guardians:
The Minotaur's Eclipse
&
The Mini Missions

◉

Moggy on a Mission

◉

Star Friend

◉

The Night I
Helped Santa

Coming Soon

Time Guardians:
The Centaur's Curse

Kinmaran Chronicles

Brackenbelly

And the
Beast of Hogg-Bottom Farm

Harry,
Live for adventure!

04/03/19

Gareth Baker

In Loving Memory of my mother, Susan Baker, who taught me the power of dreams and how to be the best human I can.

For Nicki, for all her love, support and biscuits.

One

The wind howled and chilled her bones but Isomee was determined to carry on.

Climbing the mountain was much, much harder than she expected. But she was almost at the top and once she was there she would be free — really free — for the first time ever.

Isomee's fingers reached for the next outcropping of rock. She gripped it with all her might. One last heave and she would be there.

Her body screamed with the effort and her lungs ached but, finally, Isomee scrambled over the top. She lay on her back. Although she was exhausted, her whole body was filled with excitement too. She'd done it. She'd actually done it.

Once her breath returned to normal, Isomee stood up, looked over the rocky edge and down the side of the mountain. Somewhere far below was Thorn, her faithful ride.

Isomee thought back over the last week. She'd woken up one morning, packed her things and decided to escape. After days of riding, she'd arrived at the bottom of the mountain. She'd been sad to say goodbye to Thorn but he couldn't come any further. The side of a mountain was no place for a bird, even a clever, capable one.

From the top of the mountain, it felt like she could see the whole world. After a lifetime of living on a tiny farm, Kinmara seemed to go on and on and on.

It was amazing.

In the distance, she could see more mountains. There were wide rivers that travelled across the land like snakes. There were forests. Tiny dots moved around on the land and in the sky. Then there were the cities that sparkled and winked at her in the bright sunshine. Her whole life was ahead of her, she just had to reach out and take it.

Isomee stepped forward.

And slipped on the hard, crusted snow.

Before she had a chance to stop herself, her feet came out from under her and she went sliding down a chute of ice. Down and down she went, all the time gathering speed, faster and faster until she went flying over the edge.

Isomee plummeted down with nothing but the sky below her. Cold, damp air wrapped around her as she fell through a layer of cloud. Her dress whipped around her. Her hair flapped across her face. She was falling, falling and there wasn't anything to stop her.

With a loud splash, Isomee dropped into a pool of water and sunk down to the bottom. She quickly swam to the top, her arms and legs working furiously.

As soon as she broke the surface, Isomee gasped for breath. Once she had air back in her lungs, she swept her hair out of her face and looked around.

She was in the middle of a pool of water, the bank was not too far away. The land ahead was covered in plants. There were tall trees, flowers and bushes, all bursting with colour and life. Small birds with long beaks flew up to the bright blooms and put their heads inside. The sounds of their songs and calls filled the air.

Above Isomee the sun was bright and hot. The water was warm too.

She swam for the shore and climbed back onto dry land. Water drained from her clothes, but it soon evaporated off the flat rock beneath her feet.

Suddenly she realised she couldn't swim. How? How had she done it?

In the plants ahead there appeared to be a pathway. Isomee walked toward it and one of the long-beaked birds flew over and landed on her shoulder. It tweeted and twittered softly in her ear.

Isomee reached up and the bird hopped onto her finger. They looked into each other's eyes.

"You're beautiful," Isomee said.

"And you're dreaming," the bird replied in a sweet, high-pitched voice.

"What?"

"*You* are dreaming, Isomee."

Isomee looked up, a bad feeling filling her stomach.

There came a great roar from the wall of plants. They rustled as unseen animals ran away and birds flew into the air.

"You'd better wake up, Isomee, before it's too late," the bird on her finger said, hovering up.

It looked at where the terrible sound came from and then its head darted from side to side trying to choose which way to go.

There was a sharp *crack* and a few yards away a tree laden with sweet smelling fruit crashed to the floor, flattening everything around it. Then other plants began to bend and shake. So did the

5

ground. Over the top of the leaves and petals, a mess of hair appeared.

"Wake up," came a deep, loud voice through the bushes. The plants shook and parted at the volume of the voice.

"Goodbye," twittered the bird.

It zipped off through the air. Isomee was sure its little eyes were full of terror.

She wanted to run, too, but she couldn't. She just stared and watched as a large, hairy man, carrying a club over his shoulder, came out of the undergrowth, stared at her and shouted one more time...

Two

"Wake up!"

Isomee's eyes snapped open. Their usual piercing green colour was dulled by lack of much-needed sleep. And now being woken in the middle of a dream would only make her feel worse.

It was her uncle calling, and he sounded angry. Very angry.

Isomee sat up on what she called a bed, but it was just a mattress of rushes and chostri feathers placed straight onto the cold, stone floor of her drafty bedroom. She looked at the tall, overweight man who was stood in her bedroom door. Uncle Hogg-Bottom's face looked as angry as he sounded.

"You're late," he sneered. "And because you're late and didn't wake me up, I'm late too. That means you'll have to do all the jobs I was meant to do this morning because I don't have time."

Isomee lowered her head and peeked at him through the mess of red curls that hung before her eyes. She was about to do what she always did — apologise — but he carried on ranting before she had the chance.

"That'll be on top of all your usual chores, not to mention the firewood you forgot to bring in yesterday. I can't *believe* you let the fire go out last night. What were you thinking? Can't I go to bed and leave you with a few easy jobs to do without you messing it up completely? Well, can I?"

Isomee opened her mouth to speak, but her uncle carried on.

"Well, what have you got to say for yourself?"

Isomee looked at him through bleary eyes. He was wearing his long johns and his greasy hair was sticking up in all directions. He'd obviously just got out of bed. His shaggy beard was flattened on one side where he had been sleeping on it, and the enormous pimple on his nose had finally burst. But what Isomee noticed most was the wooden bucket that hung from his hand. Through her sleep filled eyes, Isomee could see a tiny jet of water leaking out the bottom.

"I—," she began.

"I don't want your excuses, girl. I curse the day I was lumbered with you. You're no help — just extra work." He stopped being hateful and shook his head.

"I'm sorry," Isomee said, trying to stifle a yawn.

"Really?" he said. "Then you'd better show me, hadn't you?"

"Yes, Uncle."

"You can start by mopping the floor in the kitchen."

"Yes, Uncle," Isomee said, throwing back her thin, tatty blanket. The room was freezing. She really shouldn't have let the fire go out.

When she went to bed she'd slept in her clothes — a grey dress that was almost too small for her and only slightly less worn and threadbare than her pitiful blanket.

Isomee yawned again.

An evil grin spread across Hogg-Bottom's face.

"Since you need help waking up, let me give you a head start with the mopping."

He laughed.

Isomee saw her uncle move, but it was too late for her to do anything about it. He swung the bucket back and threw the ice-cold water all over her.

Through the water dripping from her hair, Isomee saw her uncle smile.

"Make sure that you do a good job of it. Remember: The uma will come and take you away if you don't do as you're told."

Three

Isomee sat on her sodden mattress and listened to Hogg-Bottom's braying laughter fade into the distance.

Water ran through her tangled hair and trickled onto her sodden dress. Now she would need to get rushes and feathers to make a new bed. The mattress would never dry out and he'd known that when he'd decided to soak her.

Isomee stood up and her cold, wet clothes clung to her. She had no others to wear so she would have to put up with it. She had no shoes or boots either. The stone floor was cold and biting against the soles of her feet, especially in winter.

"Right," Isomee said to herself. "Let's get this fire back on."

Yesterday she'd chopped wood until it was dark and then she'd stacked it against the wall under her bedroom window. By the time she'd finished, she was too tired to bring any inside to keep the fire going. Her uncle was already asleep and as the cold didn't bother him, Isomee had decided to leave it and relight the fire again before he awoke.

"So much for that plan," Isomee said.

She stepped over her ruined bed and opened the shutters that covered her glassless windows. Several of the slats that blocked the light were missing. Isomee suspected her uncle had done it on purpose. The window faced east. Most days the early morning sunlight would rush in and wake her. But not today. Today she was too tired and the sky was too grey.

Isomee looked out the window. One thing made her smile every day — even if it was a terrible day like this one seemed determined to be — and that was the view from her window. It was beautiful, especially when she was up before the sunrise.

Outside, for as far as she could see, was her farm. The fields stretched for miles, flat and endless until they reached the forest, and in the far off distance, mountains stood proudly under a blanket of snow. When she got up early enough, she could see Kinmara's sun slowly rise over the mountain. In the evening she could see the arrival of Kinmara's twin moons.

Isomee stared at the mountains and was reminded of her dream. "What's between you and the mountains," she said to the forest, hoping it would hear her question. It didn't answer.

Reaching through the window, Isomee grabbed the pile of kindling she'd left on the top of the pile of wood and went into the kitchen.

"Is that fire on yet? I need a hot drink before I check on those pointless birds," Hogg-Bottom called from his bedroom. His was the largest of the three rooms that made up the farm cottage. The kitchen separated him from Isomee. Her room was the smallest, but at least being next to the fire in the kitchen kept it warm.

"I'm lighting it now," she called back.

Isomee walked into the kitchen and carefully placed the wood on the floor in front of the fire – if she dropped it, the noise would make Uncle angry – and then walked around the wobbly kitchen table to open the shutters above the sink.

Through the window, she could see the barn. Safely tucked inside were their twelve award-winning chostri, enormous birds with long legs, long necks and a round body large enough to ride on. In fact, one of her ancestors had discovered the creatures and become rich from inventing chostri racing — or so her uncle told her. There was no sign of the money now as the house and farm buildings were left to fall apart around them.

A gentle breeze came through the empty window and carried the sounds of the chostri cawing, clucking, clicking and screeching.

"Uncle? The chostri don't sound very happy again," Isomee called.

"Have you lit that fire yet?" he called back, ignoring what she said.

"Just starting," Isomee replied as she crossed the cold floor, got some chostri feathers out of a wooden box by the fire and used them with the kindling to stack up the fire.

"You worry about getting that fire started. Let me worry about those stupid birds."

They're not stupid, Isomee thought, glaring at his bedroom door.

Isomee took a flint, which she had dug up from one of the fields, and an old knife, and began to strike the pair together. Sparks flew off the stone and landed on the chostri feathers she'd planted at the heart of the fire. They started to glow bright orange, so Isomee gently blew on them. The feathers started to burn and the tiny flames spread and began to lick at the finely chopped wood.

Now was the tricky part. The fire could easily go out before it had properly started. She couldn't afford to get it wrong.

Once Isomee was happy the fire was going and safe to leave, she went back to her room and retrieved some larger pieces of wood from the pile outside her window.

"I'd better go and check on those blasted animals," Hogg-Bottom said as he wandered back into the kitchen.

He was dressed now. Leather boots, green trousers and a woollen coat with a tall collar to block out the wind. It could blast across the flat plains and 'cut you in half' according to her uncle.

Isomee knew all about the wind. She didn't own a coat.

"Get this water mopped up or it'll seep between the stones and then the floor will start to smell. Then get my breakfast on the go. While it's cooking, bring in the wood and then you can feed the animals."

Isomee didn't have time to answer. The front door slammed as he left the house.

Putting some fresh wood on the fire, Isomee watched it for a while to make sure she hadn't accidently put it out by suffocating the flames.

The kitchen began to slowly warm up.

Now it was time to get on with everything else.

Isomee crossed to the sink and glanced out the window to get another look at the magnificent view.

Her uncle was walking across the farm towards the barn. He was muttering to himself, then, in a louder voice, he called, "Remember Isomee, do as you're told or the uma will come and get you."

Four

The cloaked, hooded figure walked along the empty road. He'd been walking since sunrise that morning. He'd been walking all week. But it didn't bother him. Uma were used to walking. Uma were used to lots of things.

Yesterday, three wagons had driven straight past him as he strode along. The drivers didn't even bother to say "Hello", let alone offer him a lift. If he'd been human, he wouldn't have been ignored — he knew that for a fact. Being ignored wasn't the worst of his problems, though.

No, uma put up with far worse.

No one — no human anyway — ever stopped to help an uma.

And why should they?

Humans were afraid of the uma. With their grey skin and pointed teeth, they looked very different from humans.

They carried disease.

They stole children.

So the carts rumbled on down the rutted, muddy tracks and the uma carried on walking. He needed to keep going. He had somewhere to be.

Later that day as the sun was setting and he was tired from ceaseless walking, he arrived at an inn. A sign with a simple painting of a bed and a mug of drink swayed above the door. The uma lowered his hood and stepped inside.

As soon as he entered, everyone stopped talking. Some got up and moved to other tables. Some left completely.

He walked further in, looking for the owner, his worn out boots stepping lightly on the creaking floorboards.

It didn't take him long to spot the owner. A man with an apron was busy delivering two bowls of soup to a couple of customers who'd remained at their wooden table. The uma could tell they were nervous. Their breath was short and fast. One of them accidently blew out the candle in the middle of their table.

"I need a bed for the night," the uma said to the innkeeper in a deep, gravelly voice. "And some of that delicious smelling soup, if you have any left."

The innkeeper put his hands on his hips and stood up as straight as he could. That was another thing uma had to put up with. They were short by human standards. By the time a human child became a teenager they were usually taller than an uma. Some humans, usually the ones most afraid, had to make a thing about being bigger than them.

"We don't serve your kind here, pointy ears," the innkeeper said. "We don't want any trouble. Why don't you just move on?"

The uma nodded and said, "I have gold."

"You could be king of all the uma and have all the gold on Kinmara for all I care. Move on before you give us all the plague."

"I'm looking for Hogg-Bottom farm," the uma said. "Will you at least tell me where it is?"

"Will it make you leave?"

"Yes, after I've had a bowl of soup."

The innkeeper nodded. "Very well. If you eat it outside, I'll draw you a map."

The uma agreed, and a short while later, with a full tummy and a map in hand, he continued to walk.

And walk.

As darkness fell, the uma stopped and slept by the side of the road. The next morning, he had a quick meal from the supplies in his pack and then headed for Hogg-Bottom farm.

He had important business there, and the sooner he got there the better.

Five

Isomee placed a fresh stack of wood beside the roaring fire. The water was mopped up and she'd thrown the rushes and feathers of her ruined bed out the window and onto the compost heap. Her only hope was that she would get the chance to make a new one while it was still light enough to see what she was doing.

She looked out the kitchen window again. The sun was up and the sky was bright and clear.

The jobs completed, for now, Isomee thought about sitting down for a moment but knew if her uncle caught her she would be in trouble. Besides, there was always something to do.

The rumbling in her stomach told her she was hungry. No doubt Uncle would be back soon and want his breakfast. In fact, she was surprised he hadn't been back already. He always spent as little time as possible with the chostri, even though they were their only source of income.

Isomee went into the larder and looked at what little food they had left. The harvest had been bad and a lot of the fruit and vegetables they'd grown had been spoiled. Uncle was supposed to go to the market to buy more, but he never seemed to find the time. It had been a while since they'd sold a chostri too. Maybe they had no money left.

On the shelf, there was a large bowl of chostri eggs. Each egg was bigger than a man's fist. There were also three jars of pickled onions and two full of beetroot. There was some strawberry jam and honey, but Uncle strictly rationed them. The bread Isomee had made two days earlier was almost used up — another job to add to her list. Finally, there was a small amount of salted bacon left. Her uncle would want that.

Isomee picked up a basket from the floor and loaded it with two eggs, bread and the bacon. Then she went back into the kitchen and put the basket down on the table.

Isomee looked at the fire. The flames had settled down and it was perfect for cooking. She picked up a long metal grid from down the side of the fire and laid it across the top of the flames. Then she reached up and grabbed a frying pan from the rack above her head. Uncle made sure she had everything she needed to care for him and the house.

There was a knock on the door.

"Who's that?" Isomee thought aloud. They rarely had visitors. They lived in the middle of nowhere and Uncle never invited people over. Isomee became excited. It must be someone who wanted to buy a chostri. She hoped so. They needed the money.

The knock came again.

Isomee put the egg on the table, took the pan off the fire and answered the door.

The figure outside was wrapped in a dust covered, mud brown cloak. A large hood concealed his face. He was only a little taller than her.

Was he a teenager?

His clothes, a dark, dull green tunic with a wide belt around his waist, looked like it had seen better days and so too did his brown leather boots, one of which had a hole where the big toe would be.

Finally, he had a sausage shaped pack across his back.

"Can I help you?" Isomee asked.

"Is this Hogg-Bottom farm?"

Isomee's eyes widened. His voice was too deep and gravelly to be a boy.

"Yes," Isomee said, peering into the darkness of the stranger's hood. She couldn't see anything. Not his face nor his hair.

He moved back and lowered his head even further, making Isomee feel a little uneasy. She hadn't met many people but this man seemed to be wanting to hide something from her.

"I need to speak to an adult. Your mum or dad," the stranger asked.

"There's only my uncle. He's in the barn. I'll go and get him for you."

"That would be most helpful," the stranger replied.

Isomee relaxed a bit. He was very polite. She stepped back, and as she did so, she unblocked the light coming from the window above the sink.

Her heart leapt into her throat and the blood drained from her already pale features. Now the light had changed, she could see inside the hood.

She slammed the door in the stranger's face.

He was an uma.

He must have come for her.

Six

Isomee's trembling fingers fumbled with the wooden bolt. She slid it across and locked the door, sealing the uma out.

Had he come because she'd let the fire go out and overslept? They were her only mistakes.

There was another knock on the door. It was louder and more insistent.

Isomee backed away, bumping into the wobbly table. The chostri eggs rolled off the top and cracked on the floor. The sharp sound made her jump.

Overcome with fear, Isomee turned and ran through the kitchen and into her empty bedroom. She hitched up her skirt and scrambled out the window. The pile of wood tumbled to the ground as Isomee fell and crashed over the top of it. The sound of ripping fabric filled the air. Isomee gathered up the front of her skirt, ignored the new tear in it, and ran across the dew covered grass, the muddy track and into the barn.

"Uncle?!" she cried as she burst through the door, her curly red hair looking like it were on fire as the bright morning sunlight shone through it.

"What is it, Isomee?" he snapped, turning from one of the enormous birds.

Isomee shrank back from his loud, intimidating voice. "Uncle, th... there's an uma at the door. Have I displeased you, uncle? Have you asked him to take me away?" Isomee said, peeping back outside in case the stranger had followed her.

"Don't be ridiculous child. Why do you say that?"

Isomee walked into the barn and stood next to her uncle.

"He's definitely an uma. He has fangs. Remember what you told me about the uma having fangs? You've sent for him, haven't you?"

The barn door creaked and it was followed by the sound of a cough.

Isomee slowly looked over her shoulder.

It was him.

The uma had come after her.

Seven

Isomee jumped behind her uncle.

"Get away from me, silly girl," Hogg-Bottom said, pushing her aside and almost sending her tumbling to the straw covered floor.

One of the chostri, Isomee's favourite, named Thorn, strutted over to her and, bending his long, slender neck, rubbed his face against her cheek. Isomee patted the creature.

Then an idea came to her. Perhaps she could escape on Thorn before the uma could grab her. Chostri were very fast. Isomee quickly dismissed the idea. Where could she go? She knew no one around here and she didn't know where any of the roads went.

Aside from the sounds of the birds eating, the barn went silent for a few moments while Isomee looked at the uma, her uncle and back again.

Finally, the stranger moved and took the pack from his shoulder and placed it on the floor.

"I've walked a long way to view your chostri. If I see one I think will suit me, I'd like to buy it. I'm willing to offer you a good price," he said from inside his hood.

Isomee stared at the cloaked uma. Was he telling the truth, or was this some trick?

"I'm afraid they're not for sale," Hogg-Bottom said.

The uma grunted.

Isomee turned and looked at her uncle. Suddenly she forgot all about her own safety. What was he on about? They had no money, no food, they needed to sell one of the birds.

Any chostri but Thorn, of course. She pulled the bird closer to her and its huge clawed feet stamped on the floor. Was the giant bird afraid of the hooded figure, too?

"I can offer you almost any sum you ask," the stranger replied. He knelt down and began to untie a pouch on the side of his pack.

"It's not to do with money—," Uncle Hogg-Bottom started to explain.

"Then what is it to do with?" replied the stranger, his voice suddenly sounding deeper and more frightening than before. He stepped forward, threw back his hood and revealed his face.

Isomee placed a hand over her mouth. Although she had seen his fangs, Isomee hadn't seen the rest of his face.

The uma's head was square and angular, with two pointed ears. His skin was grey. In his right ear was a small hoop earring. His dark, shiny hair was collected upon his head in a top-knot. Just poking out from beneath his upper lip were the two short fangs that had terrified her. His eyes were large and shaped like a drip of water tipped on its side.

"Is it because I am uma?" the stranger asked, moving his hands to his hips. The movement made his cloak slip away and revealed his bare arms and legs. They were tight and round with muscles. Around his left wrist was a leather cuff and on the right a silver bracelet.

Isomee pulled Thorn even closer and snuggled against his soft, thick feathers. He'd admitted it. He *was* an uma. He was definitely one of the child snatchers that her uncle had told her about.

But there was more.

According to her uncle, uma were liars, cheats and carried diseases. The word uma was often used as an insult. To be called one meant you were smelly or untrustworthy.

"No...no...of course not. I swear it has nothing to do with your race," stammered Hogg-Bottom as he stared into the stranger's large eyes.

Her uncle was afraid, Isomee could tell. The uma were meant to be fearsome warriors too. At least this one didn't have a weapon.

"I should hope not," the uma replied in a deep rumble.

"It's just that my flock is unwell," Hogg-Bottom began. "I'm a respected breeder and seller and I'd never sell you unworthy stock and risk damaging my good name."

Isomee hugged Thorn tighter.

"I'm sure," said the uma with a smile that revealed all his teeth, especially his fangs. "In what way are they unwell?"

Hogg-Bottom looked at Isomee and said, "I was grooming them this morning when I noticed that a couple of them had something wrong with their feathers."

"Explain," said the uma.

"They were dull. Usually, their feathers shine. It's one of the superior qualities my flock possesses."

The uma nodded.

Isomee looked at Thorn's feathers. To her relief, they looked normal.

"And when I touched them, they fell out," Hogg-Bottom continued.

"Chostri are very sensitive creatures," Brackenbelly said. "Loss of plumage is often a sign of distress. Maybe I could take a look?"

Poor birds, Isomee thought.

Before Hogg-Bottom could give him an answer, the uma strode further into the barn towards the dozen birds. Hogg-Bottom moved out of his way.

Isomee kept her arms wrapped around Thorn's neck and her eyes fixed on the strange, grey skinned man.

The uma walked up to the closest chostri, who was pecking at the ground, and said to it, "Do not be afraid."

The black feathered bird stopped what it was doing and swung its long neck up. It cocked its head to one side and looked at the uma quizzically.

The visitor smiled at the bird.

"That's amazing," Isomee whispered to her uncle. "Lavender is usually terrified of strangers."

"Shhh," Hogg-Bottom said with a finger to his lip. "It's some kind of trick. I'm sure."

Isomee stared at the stranger.

The uma held up his hand and, to Isomee's astonishment, Lavender placed the top of her head onto his waiting palm.

Now Isomee was truly amazed. Lavender was usually skittish and shy. She would often only respond to her. The bird hated her uncle. But here she was, allowing a complete stranger to touch her head.

And chostri hated having their head touched.

The stranger closed his eyes and took a deep breath.

"They're... afraid," he said.

Isomee loosened her grip on Thorn and took a step forward.

Her uncle grabbed her arm and pulled her back.

"His voice, Uncle. Listen to his voice. It sounds like *he's* the one who's afraid."

The stranger flinched and said, "At night, there's something outside... something that's trying to... get into the barn."

"How... how do you do that?" Hogg-Bottom asked in amazement.

"I thought you said it was a trick?" Isomee whispered.

"Quiet, girl," Hogg-Bottom snapped.

Isomee moved away from him.

The uma walked to his pack, took a piece of plump, ripe dew fruit from a pocket and went back to feed the chostri. The sweet smell of the purple berry filled the air.

Isomee suddenly felt very hungry.

She watched what the uma did next and was even more stunned. Lavender was eating out of his hand. The chostri wouldn't even do that for her.

"How did you do that?" Hogg-Bottom asked.

"Let's just say I have a way with animals," the stranger replied.

"I see you have discovered the truth of my little, err... problem," Hogg-Bottom said.

"Problem? What problem?" Isomee asked.

"Don't question me, girl," Uncle snapped and glared at her.

Isomee stepped under Thorn's neck and placed the bird between her and her uncle. She was afraid of the stranger, but sometimes her uncle scared her more.

"Can I show you something Mr...?" Hogg-Bottom said.

The uma stared at the bearded man, either ignoring the request for his name or not understanding the human behaviour.

"I'm Hogg-Bottom, as you know. This is Isomee, my niece," he added. "And you are? "

"Brackenbelly. My friends call me Brackenbelly. "

Eight

Isomee watched her uncle over the top of Thorn's back. He had an unpleasant smile on his face. If uma had a reputation for trickery, her Uncle Hogg-Bottom was also skilled in it. Whatever this problem was, her uncle clearly thought he'd found an easy way out of it.

"Does this mean we're your friends, Mr Brackenbelly?" Hogg-Bottom asked, rubbing his hands together.

"No, it does not," Brackenbelly answered truthfully. "I've only just met you. How am I to know if you're worthy of being my friend? Or I yours? And my name is just Brackenbelly, not Mr Brackenbelly. Now, to return to business – you wanted to show me something? "

"Yes, yes, I do. It's something outside," Hogg-Bottom said, smiling as he led the way out.

Isomee waited for them to go past her and, letting go of Thorn, started to follow. As they got to the doors, her uncle stopped and turned while Brackenbelly knelt down and collected his pack.

"Make sure you pick up any feed the birds leave on the floor, we can't afford to waste it. Then muck out their pens. Is that clear?"

"Yes, Uncle," Isomee replied meekly.

Hogg-Bottom turned his attention to Brackenbelly and said, "This is what I want you to see."

The pair disappeared outside and Isomee was left staring at the rickety barn doors. Part of her was glad she could no longer see Brackenbelly, but she also wanted to know what her uncle was showing him.

A moment later, Isomee felt a nudge on her shoulder. It was Lavender.

"Hello, girl," she said to the young chostri. "Did you like him?"

The chostri's large, black eyes stared back at her blankly.

"You weren't afraid of him at all, were you? Even when he did that thing," Isomee asked, not expecting an answer.

Through the wood of the barn wall, Isomee heard her uncle talking to the stranger.

"Shall I go and listen? What do you think, Lavender? Thorn?"

When no answer came from the two birds, Isomee crossed the barn. The straw rustled under her bare feet. Once she got to the wall she pressed her ear to the rough planks.

She could hear her uncle outside.

"I cleared it away the first few times the animal... you know... did it for fear it was marking its territory or something, but it came back each night and did it again so in the end, I gave up."

Did what? Isomee thought.

It went quiet outside and Isomee couldn't hold her curiosity back any longer. She hitched up her torn dress and rushed to the open barn door.

Isomee peeked outside and when she was confident it was safe, she stepped outside and followed the wall to the corner, where there was a stone water trough. Isomee crept up alongside it and peered over the top.

Brackenbelly and her uncle were staring at something on the floor.

It looked like...

It was!

It was a pile of animal droppings.

"And you don't recognise it? You can't tell what animal it belongs to?" Brackenbelly asked.

Hogg-Bottom shook his head.

"We have a few predators around here every once in a while, but I've never seen anything like this before."

Brackenbelly turned and Isomee ducked down below the trough. She counted to ten, her heart beating faster and faster, and then bobbed back up. If her uncle caught her not doing what she was told, there would be trouble.

In the time she had hidden, Brackenbelly had placed his pack on the ground. Isomee watched as the uma reached out for the pile of droppings with his hand. It was then that she noticed something else that was different about him. Brackenbelly had only three fingers and a thumb. It was like his little finger had dropped off. Isomee was in the middle of checking his other hand when she noticed what he was doing.

Brackenbelly was using his thumb and the largest of his three fingers to break off a small part of the large pile of dung.

He rolled and squeezed it between them. A powerful smell was released. It reminded Isomee of... It was something they didn't eat very often. What was it? Fish. Yes, it was the strong, powerful aroma of fish.

"It's still warm and moist. It's a few hours old. I suspect it was left just before dawn," Brackenbelly said. The uma stood up and looked toward the horizon. "Whatever it was, it's gone now. But why leave this here for you to find?"

Yes, why? thought Isomee.

"I don't know. Like I said, I just clear it u–" Hogg-Bottom said.

"It was a rhetorical question. I was merely thinking out loud," Brackenbelly said, interrupting him. He then brought his fingers closer to his flattened nose and took a deep sniff of the olive green mess.

Isomee wrinkled hers. If she could smell it from here, then it must be sickening close-up.

Brackenbelly flinched at its odour and coughed. He turned away from uncle Hogg-Bottom and looked straight at Isomee.

"We are being watched."

Isomee tried to duck out of sight, but it was too late.

"Why are you here?" Hogg-Bottom said.

"I've come to help," she said. Getting up from behind the trough, Isomee picked up a bucket and dunked it into the water. It was a little too heavy to lift, so she tipped some back into the trough and then walked over to Brackenbelly.

"You were told to work in the barn," Hogg-Bottom snapped.

"I brought some water for Brackenbelly to wash his hands."

"Thank you," the uma said as Isomee placed the bucket on the ground next to him. The uma washed his hands, flicked his fingers dry and then reached for his backpack.

Isomee wasn't sure who to stand next to. Uncle wasn't kind, but at least she knew him. This stranger was supposed to steal children — amongst many other things — but he'd admitted that he wasn't here to take her. And Thorn and Lavender liked him. And if Lavender liked him...

Isomee decided to stand between them both.

Soon, she found herself crouching next to the inquisitive stranger. She was sure there was something familiar about the droppings.

"Uncle, don't you think these look a little like chostri droppings?"

"Quiet, girl," Uncle snapped.

"Interesting," Brackenbelly said, untying the two yellow cords that fastened each end of his pack. He lifted the edge of the fabric slightly and slowly unrolled the bundle

Isomee stared, opened mouthed, at what she saw. The pack opened out to about a yard square. The inside was full of pockets containing who knew what.

But that wasn't all. There was a sword sat in the middle of it and something wrapped up in fine, beautifully decorated red and gold cloth. Compared to Brackenbelly's ragged appearance these objects were like treasures.

For a while, Isomee stared at the sword. Its blade looked sharp. She could tell from the many times she had sharpened the kitchen knives and the axe she used to chop the wood. The hilt was made of beautifully polished wood and the hand guard was decorated with a golden flower like the water lilies they had in the pond.

Before she could stop herself, Isomee reached out to touch the weapon. It was like her hand had a mind of its own. She *had* to pick up the sword!

At the last moment, she realised it wasn't the sword but the beautiful material she was drawn to. Her fingers were just about to touch it when a three-fingered hand gently pushed her away.

"Is something wrong?" Hogg-Bottom asked Brackenbelly.

The uma ignored the human, picked up the sword and slid it through his belt. Then he quickly rolled up the material to recreate the backpack before strapping it across his back safely out of the way.

Isomee was left staring at the ground. It was odd. She had felt compelled to reach out and touch the beautiful material, but now the fabric was hidden from sight the sensation had also disappeared. What was happening? And was it the fabric, or what was wrapped up inside it?

Isomee vaguely heard her uncle talking. Afraid she was in trouble, she looked at him.

"What is it, Brackenbelly? What's going on?" the farmer asked, his eyes darting about. "Brackenbelly? Will you answer me?!"

Isomee watched to see how the stranger would react. He held up a finger to silence her uncle and then began to follow the wall of the barn. He carefully studied the floor, perhaps looking for more droppings or other clues. He went around the end of the building and down the other side.

Isomee and her uncle followed closely behind. She tried to hold her uncle's hand but he ignored her. Like the chores he had given her, she had slipped from his mind. Isomee quickened her pace. She didn't want to stray too far from the warrior. Her uncle pushed past her.

When Isomee rounded the next corner of the barn, Brackenbelly was stopped about half way down the side. Slowly, his head moved up and down like he was examining something. Had he found another clue?

As she drew closer, Isomee discovered that Brackenbelly hadn't found any more droppings, but what he had found was worse.

Much worse.

Nine

"How long have these been here?" Brackenbelly asked, pointing at the barn.

Isomee stood next to the uma and studied what he was looking at.

Three grooves, which started just above the uma's head, went all the way down to the bottom of the wall. On the ground beneath them was a pile of long, curled wood shavings.

"I don't know. I've never seen them before," Hogg-Bottom replied.

Isomee looked carefully at the marks and said, "It looks like something's been scratching at the wall."

"Will you be quiet," Hogg-Bottom barked.

Isomee did as she was told and stepped back out of the way so that her uncle and the uma could carry on investigating.

"Yes, it does," Brackenbelly said to her. "Caused by claws, I think."

Isomee smiled at the sound of the words.

And because she'd been right.

The uma reached out and placed his fingers into the grooves.

"Something's trying to get inside. Why?" Brackenbelly asked as he followed the marks with his fingertips.

"To eat my chostri?" Hogg-Bottom suggested.

Now you like them, Isomee thought.

When Brackenbelly stepped away from the wall, Isomee moved closer and looked at the marks once again. She knitted her eyebrows together. Two were quite smooth, but one was ragged and uneven. "This one's different. I wonder why?"

"Will you stop asking stupid questions?!" Hogg-Bottom barked.

"There's no such thing as a stupid question," Brackenbelly said. "I was wondering the same thing myself. I think it might be that one of the claws is broken — snapped off and ragged."

Isomee smiled.

"I was thinking the same thing."

"Here's another good question," Brackenbelly said. "Why here? This barn's falling apart—"

"Hey," Hogg-Bottom interrupted, spraying spit into his beard and setting his hands on his hips. "There's no need to be rude. I'll have you know it's a family tradition. We build a house and rather than repair it, we build another, bigger, grander than ever before."

Brackenbelly ignored him.

"This barn's falling apart, whatever's done this could get in much easier elsewhere. I've seen several rotten patches of wood as well as loose panels on my way round. So, why here?"

"That's an excellent question," Hogg-Bottom said, changing his tone.

Isomee stared at her uncle in disbelief. She could tell he didn't have a clue as to the answer. He was just trying to get on Brackenbelly's good side.

If an uma had one, of course.

Brackenbelly started to search through the shavings.

Hogg-Bottom looked around nervously.

Isomee thought for a moment while it was quiet. Then it came to her.

"I have another idea," she said.

"If I have to tell you to shut up one more time," Hogg-Bottom snapped. Isomee looked at the floor. "Go back home and carry out your chores. "

"But I'm scared. Can't I stay here with you?"

"Perhaps you should go inside the house, just in case," Brackenbelly said, drawing his sword.

"No, I won't," Isomee said. She was scared of her uncle, but she was more scared of whatever had made the scratches.

"How dare you answer back, go to your room or..." Hogg-Bottom brought his hand up, open palmed, ready to strike her.

Isomee jumped back and flattened herself against the barn.

And braced herself.

Instead of feeling a quick, sharp pain, Isomee saw a sudden flash of light across the wooden wall.

"You will not harm the girl, sir," Brackenbelly said.

He had his sword out. It shone in the bright light. Its flat edge was pressed against her uncle's raised hand holding his arm back.

Isomee couldn't believe it. The stranger had stopped her uncle. Why would he do such a thing? She was confused. Uma were supposed to take naughty children away. She'd just disobeyed her uncle. Why wasn't Brackenbelly mad at her too?

"I'm...I'm sorry. I'm worried and not thinking straight," Hogg-Bottom answered.

The uma put his sword away and then walked towards Isomee.

Her mouth went dry. She'd been wrong. He was coming for her after all. Her uncle was right. Maybe Brackenbelly had stopped him because she belonged to him now and it was his job to hand out punishments. He was going to snatch her up under one of his muscular arms, carry her away and...

Brackenbelly stopped and knelt before her.

Isomee felt more and more confused.

Was this uma different from all the others or...?

Or had her uncle been lying to her all these years?

"Isomee," Brackenbelly said, his voice gentle. "Tell me your idea."

"I was thinking," Isomee began, her eyes flicking towards her uncle every now and again.

"Maybe it comes to this side of the barn because it can't be seen. From the house, I mean. "

Brackenbelly gently placed his hand on her shoulder.

"That's an excellent idea, and, I expect, the right answer." Turning his head to look up at Hogg-Bottom, Brackenbelly asked, "Do you ever come round here? Have you been out here at night to try and see what it is?"

Hogg-Bottom's face flashed red and Isomee knew the answer without him having to say a word. "Well... I, er, have been meaning to, but the life of a farmer is very busy and I've not found the time."

"Then that is what we will do," Brackenbelly said. "We will come out and find it. Tonight."

Ten

Isomee thought she knew exactly what her uncle's reaction would be.

And she was right.

"I'm not risking my life for a bunch of birds," he declared.

"Even though they're your source of income?" Brackenbelly asked.

"No, my life is much more important."

Isomee watched as Brackenbelly tipped his head to one side and then looked at her.

Hogg-Bottom looked flustered for a moment and then said, "What I meant to say is, well, who would look after Isomee if anything happened to me?"

"I have a proposition for you," Brackenbelly said. "I will solve this mystery and rid you of the menace in exchange for a chostri. One of my choosing," Brackenbelly said, crossing his arms over his chest.

"That seems a rather good deal — for you," Hogg-Bottom answered. "My birds are award-winners, the best in Hampdown County. I'll have you know it was my great-great-grandfather who invented chostri racing."

"That may be true, but no one's interested in chostri racing anymore, are they? I've changed my mind. I think I'll just buy one now and be on my way," Brackenbelly said as he removed his backpack and began to unfasten the yellow cords.

"Well, let's not be too hasty," Hogg-Bottom said, touching Brackenbelly's arm to stop him leaving. "How about a discount instead? A sizeable one?"

"Sounds good," Brackenbelly said. "But since I don't know what you would charge in the first place, how would I know if it's a good price?"

"Ordinarily, one chostri would cost you one hundred gold pieces," Hogg-Bottom said without the slightest pause.

Isomee's eyes widened. Her uncle was trying to cheat Brackenbelly. The last time they sold one, which was months ago, he had only charged sixty gold.

Brackenbelly didn't answer at first. Isomee realised he must have been deciding if it was a good deal or not.

"Fifty pieces? And I get my choice?" the uma finally said.

"Do we have a deal then?" Hogg-Bottom asked, his hand out ready to shake. Brackenbelly spat on his own hand, grabbed Hogg-Bottom's and shook it. Isomee could tell by her uncle's expression that it was a powerful squeeze.

The three of them followed the wall of the barn until they got back to the open doors at the front.

They went inside and Isomee started to search for left over chostri feed amongst the scattered rushes in the hopes that it would please her uncle and calm him down. There was no doubt in her mind that he would be angry with her. Maybe if Brackenbelly solved this problem for him he would be so happy he would forget about her.

Soon Isomee found herself forgetting her chores and watching Brackenbelly as he inspected all twelve of the birds.

Although her uncle had told her not to, she couldn't help but become attached to the chostri. Which would Brackenbelly choose and take with him? He'd already done that special thing with Lavender. Would he take her? Uncle was horrible to the poor bird. Maybe it wouldn't be such a bad thing.

Brackenbelly stepped up to Thorn.

Take any of them, any but that one, please, she thought.

"A good choice," Hogg-Bottom said and glanced at Isomee. She felt sure he had hatred in his eyes. How better to punish her than by selling her favourite.

"Tell me more," Brackenbelly said.

"No—," Isomee blurted, but her uncle shot her a warning look with his eyes.

Brackenbelly looked at her and then Hogg-Bottom.

"This is one of my youngest," Hogg-Bottom said. "You can tell by the comfortable, soft feathers. She's clearly not affected by our night time visitor." He patted Thorn's back, but Brackenbelly seemed more interested in the bird's legs and beak.

"Don't choose that one. Please don't choose that one," Isomee said over and over under her breath.

Brackenbelly turned and looked at her again.

Had he heard? He did have large ears. Were they extra sensitive?

Brackenbelly smiled at Isomee and she crossed her fingers. She exhaled as he moved on to the next one. Had he done it to be kind?

Or had he decided there was a better ride?

Unfortunately, the next one he looked at was special too.

"This one's Bramble. She's Thorn's mother," Hogg-Bottom said. "She's quite old."

Once again the uma started to inspect the bird's legs, beak and eyes.

"I'll take this one," Brackenbelly said.

Isomee looked down at the straw covered floor and suddenly realised she didn't want him to take any of them. It wasn't because he was an uma, but because she loved them all so much. They were the closest thing she had to friends.

"Bramble? But, she's one of my oldest. One of the original birds that my great-great-grandfather hatched," Hogg-Bottom said proudly as he stepped away from the old chostri.

"Hatched?" Brackenbelly asked.

"Yes. He rescued a clutch of abandoned eggs and brought them home. Did I mention that it was my great-great-grandfather who invented chostri racing?"

"Yes," said Brackenbelly. Isomee thought he was trying not to sound bored. Her uncle did tend to go on about it whenever he had a buyer come to view the birds.

"You're welcome to have Bramble but she's almost one hundred years old, and you can't bring her back in a few weeks and expect an exch—"

"I won't. Chostri can live for almost two hundred years," Brackenbelly said. "She's got plenty of miles in her."

Hogg-Bottom smiled.

Isomee squinted at Brackenbelly. The uma was clearly determined to have her. Bramble might have been old, but she could run extremely fast.

Could he tell that just by looking at and feeling her legs? As fast as she was, the quality that Isomee admired the most about Bramble was her loyalty. As sad as she was about it, Isomee had to admit that Brackenbelly had made a good choice.

"Do we have a deal?" Brackenbelly asked.

Isomee waited for her uncle's answer.

"It's a deal. Would you like to join us for breakfast as a sort of celebration? To seal the deal, as it were," Hogg-Bottom said, turning to look at his niece. "Isomee."

Isomee jumped to her feet and put the seed she had collected into a nearby bag. "Yes, uncle?"

"Get back home and make sure the fire's ready."

Isomee started to leave when Brackenbelly's gravelly voice came from behind.

"That's most kind, but I'd like to stay here for a while and get to know my ride. May I join you in ten minutes?" Brackenbelly asked.

"Of course," Hogg-Bottom answered. "Come along, Isomee."

She followed her uncle but looked back at Brackenbelly. Why did he want to stay behind? Was it so he could do that thing with his hand? And if it was, why was he going to do it?

Eleven

Brackenbelly waited in silence until he couldn't hear Isomee and the dreadful Hogg-Bottom anymore. The man moaned at his niece almost the whole way back to the house.

He went over to the barn doors and watched them go inside their house and then closed the battered panels. The building was plunged into darkness except where a few pools of light flooded in through holes in the roof.

Why doesn't Hogg-Bottom maintain his buildings? Brackenbelly wondered. He didn't believe the story about building a new house and farm. If they were meant to build a bigger, better one, why was their current house so small?

Brackenbelly's eyes soon adjusted to the darkness. He could see almost as well as if it was broad daylight. All uma could see in the dark, but Brackenbelly had other skills too. In particular, he had his special gift. He could sense animal's feelings, sometimes hear their thoughts and, on rare occasions, talk with them.

In hindsight, he shouldn't have used his ability in front of Isomee and her uncle, but he'd hoped to show her that he wasn't like the stories she'd obviously been told.

The poor girl had reacted with utter fear when he'd arrived at the house. It wasn't an unusual reaction to his different features, but children often had purer hearts and more open minds than adults. If only adults were more like children.

Brackenbelly looked at the chostri and smiled. Some things were not remotely afraid of him, like these beautiful birds. They gathered around him and began chattering among themselves.

Brackenbelly searched the crowd for Bramble. He soon found her. She had a dark smudge on her beak, making her easy to spot. The old chostri trotted towards him, Thorn at her side, and came to a stop.

Brackenbelly placed his hand onto his new ride's head and said, "I am Brackenbelly. I am *not* your master. I am your friend. We shall be a team. Protect me and I shall protect you. I promise to care for you and feed you. I will never abandon you. If you do not want to come with me, you may stay here. If you come and change your mind later, I will let you go. This is my solemn promise. I hope that you can hear me even if you cannot answer."

Brackenbelly removed his hand. The chostri showed no signs of understanding. He smiled. These things took time.

"Now, if you'll excuse me, I must check on Isomee."

Twelve

Isomee shut the front door.

"You just made me look like a right fool," Hogg-Bottom hissed.

Isomee stared at his yellow teeth as they flashed through his untidy moustache. She was determined not to show any fear.

"And worse still," he continued, "you've made *yourself* look like a fool. Children aren't supposed to have ideas."

He stopped for a moment and paced around the table.

"Why act in such a disobedient way? Anyone would think you wanted to be taken away."

Anywhere would be better than here, she thought.

"What's that?" Hogg-Bottom said.

Isomee's heart felt like it suddenly stopped. Had she said it out loud by accident? Had he heard?

"What's that on the floor?" he said, pointing.

Isomee relaxed a little.

"It's an egg. It fell off the table."

"Why haven't you cleaned it up? We'll get ants, or worse yet, fire centipedes, and once they get in the house we'll have to leave. We'll have nowhere to live and it'll be *your* fault."

"I'm sorry, sir. I'll clear it up straight away," Isomee said, making her way towards the mop, which was still by the sink.

"Mind that you do. I don't want Brackenbelly thinking we live like animals. We're humans, not uma. Talking of uma, Brackenbelly will be here any moment. As soon as you've cleaned up that mess, get the breakfast on. Don't be tight with the bacon. We don't want him thinking we're poor, do we?"

"No, Uncle."

Hogg-Bottom returned to his room and Isomee began to clean up. As she tidied, one thought kept running through her mind.

Why is a stranger kinder to me than my own uncle?

Isomee looked at his bedroom door and for the first time in a long time wished there was someone else she could live with. She had vague memories of her early life and she was sure it hadn't been like this.

A tear slipped from her eye. Isomee quickly pushed the thoughts of her parents to one side and started mopping. Once she was sure she had cleaned the floor properly, she got the frying pan and started cooking.

Hogg-Bottom returned wearing his best clothes and sat at the table.

"Bring me some milk."

"Yes, Uncle."

Isomee went into the larder, brought out a dented churn and ladle, and placed it on the table. Then she added three clay cups, and using the ladle, filled the first and the second. Isomee dipped the ladle back into the churn to get milk for the third cup.

Just as she was tipping it in, Hogg-Bottom nudged the table. It wobbled and the milk missed the cup and splashed all over the wooden surface.

"Clumsy girl. Well, that's your milk you wasted. None for you," Hogg-Bottom said.

Isomee went to say something when there was a knock at the door.

"Answer it then," Hogg-Bottom snapped.

Isomee opened the door. Brackenbelly was outside.

"Come in my friend," Hogg-Bottom said getting up from his seat, all smiles. "Please, sit down. I'm sorry about the milk everywhere. Isomee's just had a little accident. She's about to clear it up."

Isomee rushed past her uncle, got a cloth from the sink and wiped the table clean.

"Make yourself comfortable, Mr Brackenbelly. I'll be back once she's finished cooking. I have... something to do," Hogg-Bottom said. "Isomee, don't burn the bacon today, will you."

"No, Uncle," Isomee muttered as he disappeared back into his room.

Isomee looked at Brackenbelly as she cleaned the table. She knew she was meant to be afraid of this strange, different man, but she wasn't. He might have frightening features, but anyone who treated animals the way he did had to have a kind heart.

Isomee put the cloth in the sink and said, "Brackenbelly, how many pieces of bacon would you like with your breakfast?"

"I'm a vegetarian," he answered as he sat down at the table. It wobbled and he looked at it curiously.

"A what?" Isomee asked, putting the first slice of bacon into the frying pan and reaching for another.

"A vegetarian. It means that we, that is, uma, do not eat meat."

"Oh, sorry, I didn't know. Do you eat eggs?" Isomee asked politely.

Brackenbelly nodded.

"I'll make you a chostri egg omelette. It's big enough to feed a whole family," Isomee said enthusiastically, as she grabbed another frying pan from above her head.

Brackenbelly didn't say anything, so Isomee went about making the food in silence.

The whole time she couldn't help but think about the strange, grey-skinned uma who sat behind her. She desperately wanted to ask him questions. He said he'd walked here. Where else had he visited? Did he know what was between the forest and the mountains?

She kept silent as she cooked, her mind awhirl with questions, and then served up the food onto a wooden trencher. As she put it on the table, Hogg-Bottom burst through the door.

"Is it ready yet?" he said, sitting at the table. He looked down at the food and then, without another word, shovelled it into his mouth as if he hadn't eaten for days.

Isomee smiled.

There were bits of omelette stuck in his beard.

Isomee turned her attention to Brackenbelly. He carefully cut his food in slices and ate it slowly.

"Are you not eating?" Brackenbelly asked Isomee.

"She eats when we've finished," Hogg-Bottom answered for her.

"Why?"

"It's because I'm a child," Isomee said.

"What difference does that make?" Brackenbelly said, putting down his knife and fork.

Hogg-Bottom sat in silence.

"My uncle says–" Isomee decided to explain.

"Have you finished eating, Mr Brackenbelly?" Hogg-Bottom interrupted. "Perhaps you'd like to check the barn ready for this evening?"

"I've suddenly lost my appetite," Brackenbelly said. "Thank you, Isomee. Please, forgive me. The food was delicious."

Isomee stepped forward to clear the table and to her amazement Brackenbelly picked up his trencher and took it to the sink.

"You don't need to do that," Isomee said. "That's my job."

"Why?" Brackenbelly asked.

Isomee went to answer but the look on her uncle's face stopped her.

"I'm going out to the barn," Brackenbelly said. "Thank you once again for the delicious meal, Isomee."

Isomee's heart was filled with joy at the kind words and then sadness as she looked across at her uncle's angry face.

Thirteen

Brackenbelly was glad to be out of the kitchen and back in the fresh air.

The chostri had come out of the barn and were in the field scratching and pecking through the grass, looking for insects to eat as if they didn't have a care in the world.

And they probably don't, Brackenbelly thought, *except for whatever was terrorising them at night.*

It was Isomee he felt sorry for. The poor girl's uncle was an awful man. Why could some humans be so cruel?

Brackenbelly entered the barn and closed the doors behind him. It didn't take long for his large eyes to adjust to the dark again.

Now that he was studying the layout of the barn, he spotted that high up in the back half there was a loft. The downstairs was a large area for the chostri to shelter on rainy days. The rear half was divided up into smaller areas, or stalls, to keep each individual bird in at night or when they needed grooming.

Brackenbelly walked to the back to get a closer look at the stalls and discovered a ladder that would take him up to the loft. Right at the back, pushed up against the wall, was a large object covered in a dusty sheet.

Brackenbelly crouched down and looked under the covering. It was a machine for making fabric. He remembered that humans called it a loom. At the bottom, the weights were still there, hanging underneath it. When the loom was being used, they pulled the thread down to keep it all tight and neat. His grandmother had used an uma version of a loom many years ago to make her own fabric. This one clearly hadn't been used in years.

Moving away from the shrouded machine, Brackenbelly crossed to the ladder. He quickly climbed it. The rungs creaked with each step.

A sliver of light came through the wall and Brackenbelly saw tiny particles of dust drifting and dancing through it before they disappeared once more into the darkness. He walked through the beam of light and towards the wall.

Now that his eyes were fully adjusted, he discovered a pair of doors that were held shut by a plank of wood. Brackenbelly removed it and pulled the doors towards him.

The whole loft flooded with light as the bright morning sunshine came in. Brackenbelly turned away and shielded his eyes.

Once he'd recovered, he looked around the loft trying to find things he might be able to use to capture the mysterious night time visitor. While he had his sword, he wanted to at least try and capture whatever it was alive.

Brackenbelly returned to the door. He was certain he knew why they were there. He looked up. A rope hung above them. The other end was connected to a winch. It was used to bring things up from outside the barn and into the loft. It was also used to lower them back down.

Hung up on either side of the opening were some old nets, but aside from that, and a few rat nibbled sacks, the loft was empty.

There was nothing that could help him.

Brackenbelly leaned out of the doors and looked down. The scratch marks were to the left and about ten yards down. This would be a good place to wait for the night time visitor to arrive and then launch an ambush. The doors would give him the element of surprise, which was a good start, but Brackenbelly knew he would need a lot more than that to help him capture it.

Fourteen

Isomee finished the washing up and made sure the kitchen was clean, tidy and ready to use again later. It was what her uncle would expect. It was what she had done every day for the last seven years.

Her next task was to muck out the chostri. Luckily that wasn't such a hard job. The birds were extremely fussy and tended to use the same spot.

All of them.

Isomee thought back to the droppings outside the barn. *Didn't uncle say they always appeared in the same place?*

Isomee checked the house was the way her uncle liked it one more time, just to be sure, and went outside and headed to the barn. The morning dew had been burned off by the sun and the grass was dry beneath her bare feet.

Thorn trotted up to her as she neared the barn, and once again, she was reminded of how Lavender had responded to Brackenbelly.

Chostri were very clever birds and excellent judges of character. They all seemed to like him and he'd used that strange power of his. Surely if he were a bad man — or rather uma — surely they would have sensed it? If he was reading Lavender's mind, could she read his?

Isomee gave Thorn the attention he craved and then opened the barn. Tucked just inside the doorway were a wheelbarrow and a pitchfork. Isomee took the barrow, laid the fork inside it, and pushed it across the straw to the place where the chostri always did their business.

Fork ready in hand, Isomee was about to start when she heard the loft creak. A moment later, Brackenbelly slid down the ladder to the ground floor. He didn't seem to notice that she'd come in, either that or he was simply ignoring her.

Isomee leant on the fork for a moment and watched as Brackenbelly looked at the loom.

"It was my mum's," Isomee called.

For a while, Brackenbelly didn't react and Isomee was about to start work when he said, "Do you know how to use it?"

"No, I was too young when she..."

"When she died," Brackenbelly finished for her. Isomee nodded.

"Why are you looking at it?"

"No reason," the uma answered.

Isomee could tell he was lying. It was just an old machine, so why would he be so fascinated by it?

She put the fork back in the barrow and walked through the barn towards him.

"You were looking at the stones at the bottom."

"Yes, I was. I was thinking of using them for something, but now I know the loom's special..." Brackenbelly got up and walked towards Isomee.

"This something? Will it help you to get... you know..."

"Hopefully," he answered.

Isomee fell silent for a moment, deep in thought. The machine had sat there for years. She didn't know how to use it even though she really wanted to. Isomee thought about her mother, what little she could remember anyway, and said, "Mum would want to help us. What were you thinking of doing with them?"

"I was going to use three of the weights to make a bolas."

"A bolas?"

"Yes, it's a throwing weapon. I will also need three pieces of rope, all the same length. I'll put one of the weights on the end of each piece and then join them together. When you see your target you prepare the weapon and throw it. When it hits the target it tangles up its legs and makes it fall."

"So you don't need to kill whatever it is that's scratching the barn?" Isomee asked.

"Not if I can help it," Brackenbelly answered.

Isomee took hardly any time to consider her answer.

"You can have the weights."

"Are you sure?"

"Yes."

Brackenbelly reached into his boot and pulled out a knife. He looked at Isomee one more time and she nodded to assure him it was all right. He reached under, cut three strings and took the weights.

"There's some rope over here," Isomee said, leading Brackenbelly to the other side of the barn near to where she had listened to him and her uncle earlier that morning.

Brackenbelly took a coil of rope off the wall and Isomee sat beside him, watching him make the bolas. She smiled as his three grey fingers tied the knots ever so carefully and precisely.

"It's finished. Would you like to try it?" Brackenbelly asked.

Isomee nodded, a big smile brightening up her face.

Fifteen

Isomee and Brackenbelly went outside, walked through the flock of chostri towards the trees that were scattered in the large field outside the barn. The grass was thicker and taller and the remains of the cold morning dew soaked Isomee's feet.

"Stop," Brackenbelly said.

Isomee drew closer to him.

"Why? Have you seen something?" Her tight curls bounced and swayed as she looked left, right and then behind her, searching for whatever Brackenbelly had seen.

"There's nothing to be afraid of."

"Then why have we stopped?"

"Just wait," Brackenbelly said. Balancing on one leg, he removed first one boot and then the other.

Isomee looked at his feet. Like his hands, they had one less toe than hers. Each toe ended with a cross between a large toenail and a claw.

"Give me your foot," Brackenbelly said, kneeling before her.

Isomee lifted her leg up. He slid the first boot on and then swapped feet. They fitted her nicely and were warm and comfortable.

"You don't need to do this," Isomee said and she started to remove one.

"Please," Brackenbelly said. "Leave them on. I've been walking for days. It's nice to stretch my toes."

"Are you sure?"

"Yes."

Isomee watched as he wriggled his toes. They did look a little sore.

"Why are you being so kind to me?"

"I'm not being kind."

"Yes, you are," Isomee said.

"No, I'm not. I'm just treating you the way you deserve. With respect. The way you should be treated. Besides, you need boots. I don't. It makes sense to let you wear them."

Isomee wasn't sure if that made sense. It certainly wouldn't to Uncle. At the thought of him, she looked back over her shoulder at the house.

"Right, let's get on, shall we?" Brackenbelly got to his feet and took the bolas off his belt. "Stand back."

He began to swing the weapon above his head. Isomee could tell by his white fingers that he was gripping the rope tightly. The air started to whistle through the holes in the stones, creating a hypnotic note that got higher and higher the faster Brackenbelly swung the weapon.

"Watch the bottom branch of the tree on the right," he said, and then let go.

The weapon sailed through the air, singing as it went, and wrapped around the branch. It stopped with a loud *clack* as the stones all collided with one another.

"Now it's your turn," Brackenbelly said before he ran off to retrieve it.

When he put the bolas in her hand, Isomee was surprised by how heavy it was.

"Ready?"

Isomee nodded.

"Bring it up quickly and then twirl it above your head."

Isomee took a deep breath. She was worried. If the stones hit her in the face it was going to hurt.

Really hurt.

The moment she swung the stones up they seemed to weigh less. They began to sing as they moved faster and faster above her head.

The rope slipped from her fingers and the bolas spun off and landed in the grass behind her. Isomee looked at the ground. She'd messed it up.

She'd been distracted by the sound coming from the stones.

"Are you all right?" Brackenbelly asked.

"The sound," Isomee began, "I'd forgotten, but my mum liked to sing. The sound reminded me of her voice."

Brackenbelly got the bolas and stood in front of Isomee.

"Your mum is always with you, you know," he said. "At least that's what uma believe when the ones we love leave us."

Isomee didn't know what to say. She'd learned not to talk about her parents. Her uncle had refused to and whenever he did, it never ended well. She quickly learned to keep her thoughts to herself. Now her mum and dad seemed like a dream.

"Let's try again," Brackenbelly said with a smile.

The pair practised all morning. They moved closer to the tree as Isomee wasn't quite strong enough to throw the bolas that far. Then Brackenbelly realised it wasn't an easy target so he got a stake from the barn and hammered it into the ground.

Isomee still missed the first few times but, first one rope and a stone hit the target, and then two.

As the sun moved across the sky, Isomee got better and better and her smile got wider and wider.

Isomee stopped and wiped her forehead.

"This is hard work," she said as she rubbed her arm muscles. She leaned back to stretch out her stiff back.

Then she noticed the sun. It was almost at its highest point, bright and hot.

"Oh no! It's lunchtime and I haven't got the meal ready. Uncle will be mad," Isomee said in a terrified voice. "I better give these back too. Uncle doesn't let me wear anything on my feet."

Isomee quickly slipped off the boots, thanked Brackenbelly and rushed inside.

Sixteen

Isomee burst into the kitchen, but she was too late.

Hogg-Bottom stood there, his arms across his chest, waiting for her. His face was bright red like an over-ripe tomato. "Why isn't my lunch ready?"

"I..." Isomee began.

"I bet you haven't finished your other chores either," Hogg-Bottom added. "I saw you, wasting your time with that freak."

The door opened. It was Brackenbelly.

The bully of a man said in a gentler tone, "Just make sure they're done before tea time."

Is uncle afraid of Brackenbelly? Isomee wondered.

She felt Brackenbelly put his hand on her shoulder.

"I will help you prepare the food and complete any of your chores. Now, let's get the food ready," Brackenbelly said.

Hogg-Bottom remained sitting at the table and watched as the uma and the girl sliced up bread and got the pickles out of the larder. Isomee did it as quickly as she could. She thought she caught glimpses of Brackenbelly occasionally glaring at her uncle as he sat there and watched.

Once the food was ready, Brackenbelly insisted that Isomee ate with them. They sat in silence. As soon as the meal was finished, Hogg-Bottom disappeared, muttering something about the cellar.

"Stay there," Brackenbelly said to Isomee as he removed his leather bracer
and silver bracelet. Then he cleared the table.

"What are you doing?" she asked.

"I told you. I'm helping."

"But—"

"There is no 'but', Isomee."

She could see by Brackenbelly's expression that there was no point in arguing.

Once everything was put away they went out to the barn and completed mucking out the chostri. Isomee's muscles began to really hurt, but Brackenbelly seemed pleased to be doing some exercise.

They worked for another hour and then Brackenbelly put the pitchfork down.

"It's time to have a break," he said. "Let's have some fun."

Isomee looked across at Brackenbelly.

"Fun? What's fun?" she said, placing her tool next to Brackenbelly's.

"It's where we stop work and deliberately do something that will make us smile or laugh."

"Oh. Uncle calls that 'wasting time'," she said in a deep voice, pretending to be him.

Brackenbelly smiled at her.

Isomee smiled too. She had just done something she would never have dared to do before.

"Do you have any ideas?" he asked her.

"But there's work to do."

"From what I can remember you've done all the tasks your uncle set you."

"Then I should ask for more."

Brackenbelly smiled.

"Not today. I know. Here's something I bet you love to do — let's go out for a ride."

"But Uncle—"

"Surely I'm entitled to take Bramble out for a test ride?" Brackenbelly said, and walked over to the wall where the rope had been. A row of cobweb covered chostri halters lined the wall. Brackenbelly took two down and handed one to Isomee.

"I've been riding for as long as I can remember. I have my own halter," Isomee said. She let out a sharp whistle and called, "Thorn!"

"Bramble!" Brackenbelly said.

Isomee walked to a nearby stall and Thorn trotted after her. She took her special halter off the wall and slipped it over Thorn's head. She'd designed and made it herself.

An ordinary halter fitted over the chostri's beak and sealed it shut. Sometimes the poor birds found it difficult to breathe as they raced, so she thought of a way to keep it secured but without hurting the mount.

Isomee glanced over her shoulder. Brackenbelly had his hand on Bramble's head and was doing that special thing of his.

Returning her attention to her own mount, she tapped Thorn on the knee and the bird raised its leg up. Isomee put her dirty foot onto the natural step and swung up onto Thorn's soft cushion of feathers on his back.

As Thorn trotted out into the main barn, Brackenbelly was still fitting Bramble's halter. He seemed to be struggling with it.

Isomee waited as, finally, Brackenbelly mounted Bramble and shifted on her back. "Are you ready?" she asked.

"It's been a while since I've ridden a chostri, but I've been told you never forget."

"Let's find out," Isomee said.

Seventeen

Isomee tapped the sides of Thorn's body and the chostri trotted out of the barn door.

Looking back at Brackenbelly, Isomee noticed that he was managing very well. At slower speeds, the giant birds tended to move by hopping from foot to foot and it took the rider some time to get used to it.

Had he somehow used that special skill of his to make Bramble easier to ride, or was he already quite skilled?

Isomee suspected it was the latter. When he had inspected the birds he knew exactly what he was looking for.

Brackenbelly pulled up alongside her as they rode through the trees outside the barn.

"Where shall we go?" he asked.

"I have a race course that goes all the way around the farm. It has hairpin bends, a slalom, and even a water jump," Isomee said proudly.

"I thought you didn't know what fun was?"

"It's not fun, it's training for the birds."

"But you like to do it?" Brackenbelly asked.

Isomee nodded.

"Do you like doing the dishes?"

"No."

"Then racing *is* fun. Fun is doing the things you enjoy."

Isomee nodded.

"I *am* looking forward to racing you. I want to see who's best."

Brackenbelly laughed.

"Now that is fun, so long as no one gets upset. While the race course sounds good, I was thinking of going further afield."

Isomee looked at the house.

"I'm not allowed to leave the farm, that's why I built the course along the boundary," she said.

"Very well," Brackenbelly answered. "Show me your course."

Isomee smiled and Brackenbelly smiled back at her. It made her feel warm inside.

"It's this way." Isomee pulled on the reins and directed Thorn through the trees towards the start line.

Two poles were stuck into the ground and at the very top of each one was a flag that Isomee had sewn together from scraps of cloth.

"There are flags like this all around the course that show you where to go. Some also have arrows on. Are you ready?" Isomee asked.

Brackenbelly silently nodded.

"Sure?"

"The question is: are you ready?" smiled Brackenbelly.

If her uncle had said that, Isomee would have found the words mean and hurtful, but there was something about the tone of Brackenbelly's voice, and the twinkle in his large eyes, that showed he wasn't being unkind.

"How will we know when to start?" Isomee said. "I've never raced against anyone before."

"It's getting too hot to wear my cloak," Brackenbelly said, and he undid the ornate metal clasp that kept it pinned together and took it off. "I'll throw it up. As soon as a part of it touches the ground, we start."

"Agreed."

"Ready?"

Isomee nodded and Brackenbelly threw the cloak up into the air. It opened up for a moment, looking like a big, brown ghost, and then the tatty edge touched the ground.

"Yaaaaa!" Isomee cried and tapped Thorn's side.

They were off.

Thorn thundered ahead. As he picked up speed, Isomee could feel the ride getting smoother and smoother.

The marker for the first bend was coming up. Isomee pulled on the reins slightly and Thorn slowed down a little. He swung round the corner so close to the flag pole that it hit Isomee's leg. It hurt, but she didn't mind. She had trained Thorn to do it. In a race, every second counted.

As they came out of the bend, Isomee tapped Thorn with her knees to make him speed up again. She looked back. Brackenbelly and Bramble were right behind them.

Isomee's eyes snapped back to the front. She'd forgotten the slalom and they were almost upon it. Thorn let out a screech and Isomee pulled sharply on the reins. Then they were weaving in and out of the poles. Again they struck her on her knees, first on one side and then on the other.

Isomee was determined to win.

Next was the water jump. A tiny stream fed the pond where they got their water and occasional fish.

Thorn surged forward.

"I'm catching up!" Brackenbelly called from behind, but there was no way Isomee was going to look back again, not after what happened last time.

The stream was five, four, three, two, one yard away.

"Jump, Thorn, jump," Isomee called, and she felt the bird leave the ground. As they sailed through the air, Isomee looked down and watched as they cleared the two-yard jump. Isomee gripped with her legs ready for the landing. Thorn's two legs hit the ground and then slowed down ready to take the next bend.

"Coming through," Brackenbelly called.

This time, Isomee did look.

Brackenbelly came alongside her, Bramble's legs thundering along the main road outside the farm.

Brackenbelly looked across at her as they came side-by-side. Even the chostri were beak-to-beak.

And then Brackenbelly slowly began to slip past her.

He was in the lead.

Eighteen

Isomee bent over as far as she could and pressed her body against Thorn's back. She had to go faster. Thorn had to go faster.

How on Kinmara had Brackenbelly and Bramble managed to overtake her? Had he used his mind trick? Was her uncle right about uma being cheats? Or was he simply a better rider?

The wood and mud walls of the house blurred past her and Isomee made Thorn slow down.

Thorn swung round the pole and thundered after his mother. Isomee kept low and inch-by-inch they caught up.

She *wasn't* going to lose!

"Here comes the first hairpin," Isomee said to Thorn. "Here's our chance."

The chostri squawked back and Isomee felt the bird take control as it used its claws to slow itself right down and then whip around the pole.

They came back out the other side. They were level with Brackenbelly. The two riders looked at each other. Brackenbelly was smiling. Isomee smiled back.

Her legs hurt from gripping Thorn so tightly. Her back was stiff from bending over and the wind rushing over it. But despite all the discomfort, Isomee felt something she'd never felt before. Her heart was racing, but it wasn't because she was afraid. There was a strange feeling in her tummy like she wanted to be sick. But most powerful of all was the smile. The smile that wouldn't leave her face. Was this what Brackenbelly had been talking about? Was this fun?

Brackenbelly's eyes snapped forward and Isomee knew that the second hairpin was coming. Bramble was on the inside of the bend which would give her a shorter route, but Isomee could go faster on the outside.

"Come on, Thorn. I trust you," she said. The pair tore around the corner and overtook the older chostri and uma.

"Come on!" Isomee called again. Below her, she heard Thorn's feet pick up speed. They raced around the outside of the trees and towards the finishing line.

"I'm catching up!" Brackenbelly called, but Isomee kept staring straight ahead and rushed across the fishing line.

Isomee leant over Thorn's side and reached out with her hand. Her fingers slipped inside the hood of Brackenbelly's cloak. Sitting back up on Thorn's back, she waved the item of clothing above her head.

"Woohoo!" she cheered.

"Well done," she heard Brackenbelly call from behind her. "Let's not stop, come on."

Isomee and Thorn slowed down but Brackenbelly kept going, heading off towards the forest she looked at every morning.

Isomee looked back at the house for a moment, put the cloak on, and then followed after him.

As the house shrank away behind her, Bramble slowed down to a trot and Isomee came up next to Brackenbelly. They all came to a stop.

"Just look at those mountains," Brackenbelly said. "I used to live there, a long time ago."

"Did you, really? I've always dreamed of going there."

"Why?"

"I don't know. Just to see what's there, I suppose."

"That's the best reason there is."

"What other reason could there be?"

Brackenbelly ignored the question.

"Have you really never left the farm before?"

"No," Isomee replied. "Tell me about the world."

"What makes you think I know?"

"You said you'd walked here and that you used to own a chostri. And even if you've come from the next village, you've travelled further than me."

Brackenbelly went quiet for a moment and Isomee could tell he was thinking about the answer.

"Kinmara is a beautiful planet," he said. "It is worth exploring."

"What's a planet?"

Brackenbelly smiled but Isomee thought he looked a little sad. Was he sad for her?

"When you look at our moons, what do you see?"

"Two circles in the sky?" Isomee answered, unsure if she was saying the right thing.

"They're actually two spheres, two balls. Kinmara is also a sphere."

"Really?"

"Yes. We call this a planet. Kinmara, our planet, goes around the sun—"

"No, it doesn't. The sun goes up and down on a pole. It rises in the morning, moves across the sky and goes back down again."

"That is one idea," Brackenbelly said.

"Tell me about the mountains."

"They are very, very tall. Those mountains are almost one hundred miles away. We've ridden, what? Maybe half a mile.

"How many is one hundred. I...I can only count to twelve. My uncle taught me so I could put a dozen eggs or beetroot in a bag so he could sell them at the market."

"One hundred is ten lots of ten. Imagine ten chostri eggs in a row. And then imagine ten lots of that next to each other.

"That's a lot."

"Yes," Brackenbelly agreed, "and a mile is a lot bigger than an egg. I think we should get you back home, don't you?"

"Yes, but can we ride next to each other so I can ask more questions."

"Of course," Brackenbelly said, and they started heading home.

Nineteen

Isomee enjoyed the steady rhythm of Thorn's trot.

There were so many things she wanted to ask Brackenbelly, but one thing, in particular, had been burning away at her since he first came to the barn.

"Can I ask you a personal question?" Isomee said.

"Ask me. I don't have to answer."

Isomee suddenly felt embarrassed. Was the question she wanted to ask rude?

"Go on," Brackenbelly said encouragingly.

"How can you read an animal's mind?"

"I... I have a gift," he said.

"A gift?" Isomee asked.

"Yes. Not everyone has one, just a few... special people."

"Special people?"

Brackenbelly nodded. "The uma call us The Chosen, or in our language, the Fal-Muru. "

"Chosen for what?" Isomee asked.

Brackenbelly let out a short laugh.

"No one really knows, but an old prophecy speaks of the Fal-Muru uniting together to defeat a great evil."

"Can only uma be Fal-Muru, or can humans too?" she asked.

"I don't know, I only know of myself, a handful of other uma and the prophecy. Why are you so interested?"

"Isn't it obvious? I wish I could do something like that," she said, letting go of Thorn's reins, holding out her hand and mimicking the uma.

"You shouldn't," Brackenbelly said.

"Why not?" Isomee looked across at her companion, trying to read his strange and unusual face.

"It hurts. Now, let's leave it at that," Brackenbelly said.

"When you use it?"

"No more questions," Brackenbelly said. He was smiling, but Isomee could tell he didn't want to talk about it anymore. "Race you home?"

Isomee smiled and didn't answer. Instead, she tapped Thorn's side with her knees and shot off.

Once they were back at the barn, they gave all the chostri some food and made sure that Bramble and Thorn had plenty to drink.

Then they headed to the house.

They washed their hands and face and began to prepare the evening meal.

They were putting it on the table when Hogg-Bottom arrived. His mood was no better than earlier.

"Hope you realise I'm not paying you for all this work you've been doing," Hogg-Bottom said. "Or giving you any additional discount off Bramble."

Isomee smiled inside. He'd obviously been busy all afternoon and didn't have a clue they'd sneaked off.

"Don't worry, I'm doing it for the girl, not myself, and certainly not for you," Brackenbelly answered as he dumped Hogg-Bottom's trencher of food in front of him, spilling some of it onto the table.

The farmer scraped his chair back and left without saying another word.

"Please, don't upset him. You'll only make him... worse," said Isomee.

"Why don't you leave this place? Leave that... that... man."

Isomee listened to what the uma had to say and thought about it. For the first time in her life, she was beginning to question her relationship with her uncle. Was the way he treated her wrong?

"Maybe it's different for uma children," Isomee said. "But for humans, we serve our parents. It's how we learn humility. It's how we learn to be good adults."

"Is your uncle a good adult?" Brackenbelly asked her. "Children should respect their parents and help them, yes, just as I help and respect you. But children should play. Have friends. Should learn by going to school and having good role models."

"I... I recall some of those things. It's hard to remember, but my life wasn't always like this. Before my mum and dad died, life was...different."

"You see."

"I was only little, though," Isomee said. "I was too young to help around the house."

"And now you do it all while your uncle lazes around. He has no idea we left the farm and went for a ride. Anything could have happened to you."

"That's the way of things. He worked hard when he was a child. Now he gets his reward of being able to sit back and relax. I'll get my reward later when I have children."

"Oh, Isomee," Brackenbelly said, shaking his head. "I may be a different race to you, but I have known human families — good human families — and this is not how it's supposed to be. We don't control each other. We help each other."

"Even if what you say is true, he's still my uncle and this is my farm — or it will be one day. I can't leave *it*, so I can't leave him."

Isomee abruptly turned around. She was crying and didn't want Brackenbelly to see her. He was only trying to be kind, but somehow his words, his ideas, just made her sad.

Isomee heard a chair scrape across the floor.

"It's getting dark. Stay inside. I'll put the chostri away. I'll see you in the morning," Brackenbelly said, and with that, he was gone.

Twenty

Brackenbelly found putting the chostri away harder than he expected.

They were fast — that was why he wanted one after all — intelligent and they also liked to play jokes and wind people up like an eight-year-old boy.

Brackenbelly decided it was time to start thinking instead.

He walked to the barn, ignoring the birds, and shut one of the doors. As soon as he began to close the other, the twelve birds scampered towards him, keen to get inside out of the dark and whatever would be coming later. It was exactly what Brackenbelly hoped would happen. The

mind was always more powerful than the sword –
or a bolas for that matter.

Now that it was dark outside, the barn was
completely black inside. Even his large eyes
wouldn't become accustomed to the complete
absence of light.

He crouched in the darkness, removed his pack
and un-toggled one of the pouches on the outside.
His fingers dipped in and came out with a piece of
golden moss. It fitted nicely into his palm. He put
his hands together, trapping the moss inside, and
rubbed them against each other as if he was
making a ball of dough.

A few moments later, light began to leak
through the gaps in his fingers and when he
separated his hands again the moss sat there
emitting a powerful glow.

It was an uma invention called illumi-moss.

Brackenbelly collected his belongings up and
holding the illumi-moss up high, walked to the
back of the barn. He climbed the ladder, took one

of the nets off the wall by the doors and used it to make a hammock.

He settled down for the night.

◉

When Brackenbelly awoke hours later, the moss had only the faintest of glows left. It was time to see what was outside and trying to get in.

Sitting up in the hammock, Brackenbelly peered down at the sleeping chostri on the ground floor. He'd forgotten to put them in their stalls, but while he couldn't quite see them, he could tell by their breathing that they were relaxed, peaceful and fast asleep.

Hopefully, they'd stay that way.

Brackenbelly picked up his sword and bolas and tucked them through his belt.

His plan was to open the two delivery doors and wait and see what happened next. It was as simple as that. It wasn't much of a plan, but until he knew what he was dealing with he felt there was little point in planning too far ahead.

Brackenbelly swung the doors open as slowly as possible so they wouldn't make any noise. It was still dark outside but now that the double doors were open moonlight flooded in. His eyes expanded and he could make out most of the details of the landscape beyond.

After a quick search, he stepped back so that he was hidden in the darkness. For all he knew, the creature could have superior vision like himself or maybe a heightened sense of smell. He hoped that by sleeping in the barn all night his scent would be disguised by the smell of straw and the chostri snoring below.

Brackenbelly swept his eyes across the land outside, but there was nothing. Had he missed it?

He stood and searched until his legs started to ache. In the far off distance, the first rays of sunlight were starting to peek over the horizon. It, whatever it was, obviously wasn't coming tonight.

"Time to go back to bed," he said to himself.

Then he saw it.

A movement among the trees where he and Isomee had been practising with the bolas the day before.

Brackenbelly shifted his position a little so he had a better angle out of the door for viewing whatever it was. It moved quickly from tree to tree even though it was too large to conceal itself behind them.

Brackenbelly could only make out a vague shape, but it looked surprisingly familiar - two legs, a round body and a long neck.

Then he felt like kicking himself. When he and Isomee had cleaned out the barn he should have noticed how familiar the droppings were.

The approaching creature made its final dash across the open grass to its nightly visiting place.

Brackenbelly could finally see it properly. It looked just like one of the chostri from downstairs, or at least it had once. Now it was different, darker, somehow more frightening.

The soft parts of the feathers had fallen off leaving only the hard cores. It made it look like a strange hedgehog or a porcupine with two long legs. The claws, which were usually short and helped the bird grip and run, were long, sharp and ragged. One was broken just as he and Isomee had guessed.

Brackenbelly had seen animals like this before. They'd gone feral. Maybe the chostri had been domesticated once, but it had been left to fend for itself and returned to its wild ways.

Maybe it had even gone a little mad.

Brackenbelly felt sorry for the creature. He had to try and capture it and use his special gift to find out what had happened.

There was only one problem — there was no telling what it might do when he tried.

Twenty-One

Isomee couldn't sleep.

Her mind was just too active. She couldn't stop thinking about all the things that Brackenbelly had been teaching her, even if he didn't mean to, and telling her. There were so many more questions she wanted to ask about Kinmara.

Brackenbelly had said there were other planets. Were there people living on them, too? Were there ways of getting to there?

She snuggled down into the fresh mattress she had made after dinner and pulled the blanket tighter around her. If she warmed up, perhaps she would drop off again.

Isomee felt sleep taking over her when a terrible grinding sound tore through the night. She knew exactly what it was. Throwing off her blanket, she leapt to her feet and ran out of the house.

Brackenbelly might need her help and she was determined to give it.

Brackenbelly watched as the creature came to a stop at the wall. Its right foot came up and the long, gnarled claws bit into the wood. It raked them down it with a single, powerful stroke.

For a moment, Brackenbelly couldn't take his eyes off the claws. Each was as long as his forearm. They made a dreadful sound as they went about their work.

How had Hogg-Bottom not heard the deep, piercing noise? Brackenbelly wondered. *Maybe*

he had but just chose to ignore it like the coward
he was.

Brackenbelly reached out and unhooked the last net from the wall, all the while keeping his eyes fixed on the feral chostri outside. He felt for the drawstring that pulled the net closed, got his knife from his boot and sliced through it. He shook the net until it opened to its fullest extent. Then he reached down and slid the knife back in his boot.

Holding the net up, he moved as quickly as he dared to the edge of the door and threw it down towards the great bird.

Then he kicked the handle on the winch to release its mechanism, leaned through the open doors and jumped out with the rope held tightly in his hand.

Isomee hadn't expected the ground to be quite as cold as it was as she raced across the grass towards the barn. The creature had arrived and if she was right, fighting it would be the worst thing Brackenbelly could do.

He said he only wanted to catch it, but even that seemed unfair in the circumstances. She was sure she'd worked out what it was, she just didn't know why it was coming at night. She had to get to Brackenbelly before it was too late to help him, or save the poor, miserable creature.

Brackenbelly didn't plummet straight down as he leaped out of the door high above the chostri. Holding the rope with his left hand, he used it to slow his fall so he could run down the wall.

As he got closer to the chostri, he was pleased to see the net had done its job and fallen over the bird, trapping it. It screeched out in anger and attacked the net with its beak, tearing at it frantically.

Brackenbelly was almost at the bottom of the wall. It was time to put the next part of his plan into action.

Returning both hands to the rope, he jumped, pushing himself away from the wall and out into the air.

Brackenbelly jarred to a stop as the winch ran out of rope. He slowed down and began to swing back towards the wall, and more importantly, the trapped chostri.

He hit the feral creature, knocking the bird off its feet. The bird squawked as it rolled about on the floor, becoming more entangled in the net.

Brackenbelly dropped to the ground, the impact with the bird knocking the wind out of him. He shook his head and staggered to his feet as he grabbed the rope. If he could use it to tie the two sides of the net together, the bird would be trapped and he wouldn't have to hurt it any further. Then all he had to do was put his hand on its head and try to communicate with it. Talking was always the best way to solve a problem.

The feral bird, however, had different ideas. It pushed against the netting with its powerful legs and the claws did the rest. First one side of the net and then the other were shredded, leaving it hanging around the bird in useless tatters.

Before Brackenbelly could jump out of the way, the chostri rolled around on its back and flipped onto its feet with one swift, fluid movement. With a flick of its neck, the net flew free and landed over Brackenbelly. The chostri moved closer and let out a quick, vicious kick at him.

Brackenbelly brought his left arm up to protect his face, bringing the net up with it.

The gnarled claws sliced through the pieces of rope as easily as Brackenbelly had sliced through Isomee's tasty omelette, but the sturdy leather bracer on his arm managed to stop the claws doing the same to him.

While it prevented the damage, it didn't stop the impact. Brackenbelly was hurled to the ground. When he came to a halt, he rolled across the floor leaving the destroyed net behind him.

The chostri lifted its neck to its full height and drew back its head ready to strike. The head snapped forward and Brackenbelly rolled out of the way.

It was close. Too close.

"Wait! I don't want to hurt you," Brackenbelly said, holding his left arm out and wishing he could talk to it.

The bird's head snapped forward again, like a snake striking at its prey. Brackenbelly scuttled backwards on his hands. The bird missed, but immediately charged and struck out with its claws.

He didn't want to, but Brackenbelly drew his sword and brought it up to defend himself. Two of the chostri's claws were sliced off by its razor sharp edge. They spun off in the air. One embedded itself in the ground near Brackenbelly's head and the other thudded into the barn wall near the marks it had once made.

The feral chostri withdrew for a moment, keeping its eyes firmly locked on Brackenbelly and his sword.

"I don't want to hurt you," Brackenbelly tried again and lowered his sword.

But the feral chostri didn't take any notice. With surprising speed, the bird rushed in again, snapping at Brackenbelly with its beak.

The uma moved fast too. He rolled one way and then the other, fending off the furious beast with his sword. As he ducked and dived, Brackenbelly spotted a movement from the far end of the barn.

It was the worst thing that could have happened.

It was Isomee.

Isomee poked her head around the corner of the barn. She'd been right about what she thought the creature was, but she hadn't expected to find Brackenbelly on the ground and at the mercy of the angry chostri.

She had to help him, just as he would have helped her.

Isomee jumped around the corner. "Hey!" she shouted as she waved her arms around. "Over here."

The featherless chostri lashed out at Brackenbelly one more time and then turned to face her.

It looked angry. It looked ugly. It looked evil.

Isomee immediately felt bad. If she'd learned one thing from Brackenbelly, it was to not judge people by their appearance. The memory of her first reaction to him flashed through her mind.

Now she was trying to save him.

"I think I know what you want," Isomee called. "Come with me and I'll let you have it."

The giant bird appeared to nod its head and slowly began to trot towards her.

Isomee let out the breath she didn't even realise she'd been holding.

"I can do this," Isomee whispered to herself. Feeling confident, she began to walk towards the chostri.

The large bird stopped walking and Isomee thought that perhaps she had scared it. Then she noticed it was sniffing the air. It let out an ear piercing screech. Isomee was forced to cover her ears as the sound filled the night around her.

Then the chostri charged.

The creature was incredibly fast.

Before Isomee had a chance to dive back around the corner of the barn, the bird collided with her, sending her flying. She saw the stars in the sky for a moment and had just enough time to think they were pretty, when the whole world around her went black.

Twenty-Two

Brackenbelly ran faster than he'd ever run before.

The giant bird moved over to Isomee's unconscious body and forced its head under her back. Using its claws to push itself forward, the chostri worked its way under her until it was able to bring its head up and roll her onto its back.

And then it ran, carrying Isomee away with it.

Brackenbelly snatched the bolas from his belt and began to swing it above his head. The chostri was getting away and with each step, it was increasing its lead.

It was now or never.

He let the bolas go.

It flew after the fleeing bird. The three weights sang their high pitched whine.

The noise caught the feral chostri's attention and it jinked to the right at the last moment.

The weapon went flying past the fleeing creature and wrapped itself around the post Brackenbelly and Isomee had been using earlier.

The bird looked back over its shoulder and let out what sounded to Brackenbelly like a laugh.

The uma clenched his fist in frustration and burst into a run. By the time he made it to the barn door he realised that missing the beast was actually a good thing. The chostri had been moving fast and if he'd managed to bring it down there was a good chance that Isomee would have been seriously hurt when she was thrown from the trapped creature.

Brackenbelly threw open the barn doors and heard the chostri scamper to the back. He needed Bramble and quickly. He cleared his mind and sent out calm, friendly emotions hoping the link he had started making earlier would be powerful enough to bring the chostri to him.

Thank goodness he'd gone out for that ride with Isomee. That would have strengthened the bond too.

"Bramble, it's me, Brackenbelly. We must go. We must help Isomee," he whispered. Within a few heartbeats, a shape emerged from the gloom and formed into a chostri - his chostri. Brackenbelly recognised the black smudge on her beak.

Bramble trotted up next to him and Brackenbelly tapped her knee. She raised it up forming the step. Brackenbelly put his foot on it and swung himself onto the soft natural saddle of feathers. Bramble wasn't kitted out with reins but there wasn't time to put them on. Brackenbelly was certain his strong legs could grip the bird. He only hoped they weren't already too late.

"Let's go," he said, and gave the bird a firm, but gentle, squeeze with his thighs. Obeying the command, Bramble shot out the door.

Daybreak was fast approaching as they raced through the trees outside. They dodged left and right as they wove through the winding path of tree trucks and after the featherless fiend.

Brackenbelly directed Bramble towards the stake where the bolas hung wrapped around it.

"Come on, Bramble. I know you can do it. Look for Isomee," Brackenbelly said. He hoped Bramble would find a scent trail to follow. Chostri had an excellent sense of smell.

Bramble sniffed the air, her head swaying from side to side as she tried to track it down.

Suddenly she stopped.

She'd found it.

Brackenbelly smiled.

"Come on, girl, we've a job to do," Brackenbelly said, and Bramble surged forward following the trail her clever beak had found.

They were moving so fast the wind rushed through Brackenbelly's hair, forcing him to squint his eyes as dust and leaves flew up into the air.

"Faster, girl, faster. We need to get to Isomee before it's too late," Brackenbelly said.

As if from nowhere, Bramble seemed to find a little more speed.

With Bramble doing all the hard work of following the trail, Brackenbelly tried to figure out what was going on.

He'd been on the floor and almost beaten, so why hadn't the feral chostri finished him? Why take Isomee and run?

Brackenbelly's thighs began to ache from gripping Bramble's flanks. He shifted position slightly, bringing a protest from the chostri, and noticed that the sky was getting lighter by the second. Soon Hogg-Bottom would be up and letting his flock out. Maybe he would notice Isomee was missing, but Brackenbelly knew that even if he did, he was very unlikely to help.

They had been travelling for at least a mile when Bramble began to slow down and Brackenbelly risked looking up.

He was surprised to find they had arrived at the remains of an old house. A few sections of the walls were still intact. Grasses grew out of the rotten window frames and wild flowers adorned the ragged tops of the stone walls, making it look strangely beautiful.

Brackenbelly swung his leg over Bramble's back and dismounted her by sliding down the silky feathers. He patted her and walked through what had once been the house's garden.

"Why has it brought Isomee here?" Brackenbelly wondered aloud and glanced back at the bird. "And more importantly, where exactly is she?"

Brackenbelly drew his sword and entered the remains of the house through a crumbling door frame. The smell of rotten wood and damp soil wriggled up his nose like a determined worm.

The floor of the house had been totally taken over by nature. Weeds covered most of it, the most dangerous being some poisonous purple stinging nettles.

It was when he moved away from the potentially dangerous plants that he noticed it.

There was a beaten down path made from demolished floorboards and packed earth that started in a gap in the crumbled wall. It led to a rectangular opening in the ground.

It was a staircase that went under the house.

Brackenbelly had a terrible feeling that was where he'd find Isomee.

Twenty-Three

Brackenbelly returned to Bramble and took her head into the palm of his hand. He closed his eyes so he could concentrate and hoped that this time his special link would allow him to talk with her.

"If I don't come back, run," he said. "If the feral chostri appears, run. If Isomee finds you, take her and run."

Brackenbelly didn't know if she understood, but Bramble rubbed the top of her head into his palm like a cat.

Hoping Bramble had understood, Brackenbelly headed back into the ruins of the house. For a few moments, he stood at the top of the shadowy staircase. He was ready to fight the mad creature if he had to, but the most important thing was getting Isomee to safety.

He looked at Bramble one more time, gave her a quick nod of reassurance, and descended into the darkness.

Who used to live here? And why did they have such a deep cellar? he wondered as he went down the stone steps.

His thoughts were suddenly interrupted by a dreadful smell. He'd sniffed it before, but this time, it was stronger - much stronger. It was the almost overpowering reek of the droppings that had been left by the wall of Hogg-Bottom's barn.

So this *was* where the chostri had come to! But why?

As he descended the stairs, Brackenbelly hoped the smell wouldn't get any worse. The pile the stench came from must be huge, he realised. When he reached the bottom of the steps, it was almost completely dark and he wished he'd brought his golden, light-giving illumi-moss with him.

So he could find his way, Brackenbelly held his sword in one hand and stroked the other along the stone wall. It felt rough and angular as if it had been carved out of the rock.

Why would someone make all this effort to dig through solid rock? Had this been a mine? Was that why the house had been built?

The passage began to get wider and Brackenbelly saw a dim source of light ahead. Soon he was able to see more clearly.

Brackenbelly walked for a few more yards, stopped and looked in amazement. In front of him was a cavern, and it was huge. Hogg-Bottom's barn would easily fit inside it four times.

So that answered one question. The tunnel must have been dug so whoever used to live here had access to this enormous space.

Grey, early morning light streamed down from a ragged, gaping hole in the roof. Below it was a large pile of boulders, rocks and stones. Snaking down from the hole were large, thick roots that dangled and swayed as if desperately seeking water.

"The roof's caved in at some time," Brackenbelly whispered. "I must be careful. This whole cave could be unstable."

Brackenbelly stepped into the wide, open cave and began to search for Isomee. Below his feet a layer of the disgusting dung squelched against the soles of his boots. The filth covered most of the floor. As he moved closer to the cave's centre, something on the floor caught his eye.

Footprints.

Chostri footprints.

And they definitely belonged to the one he was following because one print had no claws.

Brackenbelly looked up. It was time to see what was on the other side of the pile of rocks. That had to be where Isomee was.

Isomee woke.

Her throat was in agony and she was desperate for a drink. It was as if something was burning inside her. Then the smell hit her. It was vile and she recognised it straight away.

Sitting up, she quickly looked for the feral chostri.

She was inside a cave sitting next to an enormous pile of rubble. The bird was nowhere in sight. How long had she been here, breathing the disgusting air?

Too long. Isomee got to her feet and wasting no more time, began to walk around the bottom of the pile.

Spotting something on the other side, she quickly crouched down. It was too dark for her to see who it was, but she soon realised it was the wrong shape to be the bird.

"Brackenbelly?" Isomee called.

"Yes, it's me," came his familiar, deep voice. "Don't say anything else, just get here as quickly as you can."

Isomee ran towards him and was almost by his side when from behind her, she heard the clattering of stones.

"Don't look back, Isomee, just run!" Brackenbelly called.

But despite the warning, she stopped, turned and looked up at what he must have already seen.

The feral chostri was standing at the very top of the mountain of stone, and it didn't look happy to see its prize escaping, or the invader who was in its home.

The bird let out a screech so loud that Isomee had to clamp her hands over her ears.

Brackenbelly was calling out to her — she could see his mouth moving — but all she could hear was a painful ringing in her ears. He lifted his arm and beckoned her towards him.

Isomee looked back at the chostri one more time and saw it lift its three-clawed foot.

It stamped it down as hard as it could.

At first, nothing happened, and then the cave was filled with a deep rumbling as an avalanche of rocks and stones tumbled down the pile towards her.

Twenty-Four

Brackenbelly had started to run towards Isomee before the chostri had even caused the rockslide.

He pushed his body and his short legs harder. He needed to get to her before it was too late. There was no way to stop the rocks now. His only choice was to remove her from their tumbling, rumbling path.

She was just a few more paces away when a blur flashed before Brackenbelly's eyes and the ground shook, making him stagger.

The feral chostri had landed between him and Isomee. It must have used its strong legs to fire itself up off the top of the rocks and into the air.

"All I want is the girl," Brackenbelly called, stepping away from the creature.

The bird opened its beak and in reply let out a terrible, high-pitched scream.

Brackenbelly searched for Isomee through the cloud of dust that hung in the air, but she was nowhere to be seen.

And that was when the chostri attacked. Brackenbelly jumped back and used the sword to keep the bird at bay.

"Come on then," he yelled, exposing his fangs.

If he could get the bird angry and focused on him, maybe it would forget about Isomee and she could escape.

Isomee ran to the side. She wasn't going to just stand there as the rocks tumbled towards her.

Then she stopped as the chostri landed. She had to check on Brackenbelly. Several rocks bounced past as the cloud of dust rolled over her, blocking out the chostri, and more importantly, Brackenbelly.

Isomee wanted to call out but she thought that Brackenbelly was distracting the bird so she could escape.

She had to make the most of it. He could take of himself. Isomee started to move when she heard the piercing cry of the feral chostri.

Could she really hide and leave her friend? Could she run and let him hurt the bird and make a terrible mistake?

◎

Brackenbelly stepped to the side as the bird attacked with its claws and beak. He slipped in the filth on the ground and fell, only just managing to keep hold of his sword.

He rolled away as another strike came at him. Brackenbelly tried to scramble to his feet but he couldn't get a grip on the slick floor. The smell from the droppings grew worse and worse as he churned their foulness up.

Brackenbelly quickly scanned the cave. The cloud of dust had finally begun to clear but Isomee was still nowhere to be seen. Hoping that she'd escaped, Brackenbelly got to his feet and ran towards the rock pile.

As soon as he reached the bottom, he leapt up and began to climb the unstable mound of rocks and boulders. It was steeper than it looked and the smaller rocks tumbled away under his feet, making it more difficult to climb.

The bird's sharp screech gave Brackenbelly just enough time to dodge as it suddenly appeared behind him.

Then disaster struck.

His sword slipped from his fingers and he was forced to watch as it slid between the bird's legs and continued all the way down to the bottom of the pile.

Brackenbelly rolled to the side just as the bird attacked with its foot. Thankfully, it was the one with no claws.

Water dripped from the twisted roots that dangled from above and splashed on Brackenbelly's forehead, giving him an idea.

Turning his attention back to the mad bird, he kicked out and caught it in the knee, making it stagger and fall all the way back down.

Brackenbelly reached up, grabbed the root and used it to haul himself back to his feet. He climbed further up the pile, took hold of the thick root in both hands and waited for the bird to begin climbing back up.

It charged back up the pile, screeching and snapping its beak.

When the chostri was in range, Brackenbelly swung on the root and tucked himself into a tight ball. He sailed through the air and over the top of the charging chostri.

He looked back and watched as it frantically tried to slow down, stumbled and fell to its knees.

Brackenbelly swung back. As soon as he was in range, he kicked at the chostri.

The feral bird screamed wildly as its round, featherless body rolled back down the mound.

Brackenbelly let go of the root, landed on the steep slope of the rocks and looked down at the bird.

It didn't move again.

Confident the chostri was beaten, Brackenbelly slowly made his way down the pile.

Isomee rushed forward but she was too late to stop Brackenbelly from hurting the bird.

She suddenly felt very sad. It wasn't the chostri's fault, any of this.

What had she and Brackenbelly done?

What had her family done?

It was her fault. She should have shouted a warning and stopped him.

As she got closer, Isomee saw Brackenbelly reach out towards the bird. Did he feel bad, too?

No, he was reaching for the sword that was lying next to the chostri!

Had he decided to kill the creature after all?

"Brackenbelly! Don't!" she cried out.

He turned to look at her.

"It's all right. I'm not going to hurt it," he said. "I—"

A screech filled the air and Brackenbelly turned back to face the poor chostri.

Seizing its last chance to attack, it struck at Brackenbelly's outstretched hand. He had just enough time to pull it back out of the way.

The beak missed by the width of a chostri's feather and instead of the beak biting his fingers, the top of the creature's head touched Brackenbelly's palm.

There was a loud *crack* and something terrifying and amazing happened.

Twenty-Five

Isomee watched as the chostri and Brackenbelly suddenly flew apart from each other.

The old bird slid across the floor, while Brackenbelly travelled through the air and crashed into the pile of rocks.

"Brackenbelly? Can you hear me?" she asked, crouching at his side.

When no answer came, she bent down close to his face and listened to the sound of his breathing.

Thank the gods of Kinmara.

He was alive.

She'd finally found a friend. She couldn't lose him now.

What had happened? Why had Brackenbelly and the chostri been thrown apart like that?

Isomee was fairly sure she'd seen him touch the chostri's head. Had he tried to use his gift and it had gone wrong?

Certain that Brackenbelly was still breathing, Isomee went over to the fallen chostri.

It was unconscious too. Somehow it didn't look frightening anymore. Instead, it looked sad and lonely, like her.

From behind, Isomee heard tumbling stones. She turned and saw Brackenbelly slowly sitting up at the bottom of the pile.

"Brackenbelly, thank goodness!" she said.

She ran over and threw her arms around him.

"Are you all right?" she asked.

"I have a terrible headache, but yes. Are you?"

Isomee nodded.

"What happened?"

"I accidently made telepathic contact with her. I wasn't ready and her feelings were so intense that we were thrown apart by a concentrated blast of psychic energy."

Isomee nodded, though she didn't understand most of the words he used.

"Is the chostri all right?" Brackenbelly asked.

"I'm not sure."

"Let's go and find out."

The bird awoke — perhaps it had sensed their presence — and floundered on the floor, one leg kicking wildly while the other lay twisted and still.

"The poor thing's hurt," Isomee said as they both rushed over to it.

"Easy girl, easy," Brackenbelly said as he knelt beside the chostri and cradled its head in his lap.

She didn't lash out at him.

Maybe she knew she was hurt and couldn't fight on anymore, or, Isomee hoped, perhaps she could sense that they wanted to help her.

"Do your thing," Isomee said. "Tell her it's going to be all right."

Brackenbelly nodded.

"Give me your hand, too. Maybe I can extend the link."

Isomee held out her hand and Brackenbelly put it on the chostri's head.

"It will be safe, I promise," he said.

"I know. I trust you. Besides, I want to help her."

"So do I, Isomee. So do I. Ready?"

Isomee nodded and Brackenbelly put his hand on top of hers.

Nothing happened for a moment and then something wonderful but heart-breaking began. She was seeing into the chostri's memory!

Isomee's mind was flooded with images and it wasn't long before she knew she had guessed correctly about the chostri's identity.

She'd only left the nest for a few moments. Her husband had gone hunting so they had something to eat. But he was gone so long. She was hungry and thirsty. The river wasn't far. Fifty paces at most.

Fifty there and fifty back. A total of one hundred paces.

What could go wrong?

When she returned to the nest, her world cracked open.

Her eggs were gone. Gone! She dashed about. Panic seized her. She looked and looked but there was no sign of her precious eggs.

"My babies, where are my babies?" she squawked.

And then she knew. She caught the scent of a man and saw his foot mark in the soil.

A man had been and taken her babies.

Isomee felt the heat of the tears running down her face.

Brackenbelly had them too.

"Why are we crying?" she asked.

Brackenbelly looked at the old chostri.

"We're channelling her feelings as well as her thoughts. These tears we're shedding are hers. It will pass." Brackenbelly went quiet.

"What is it?" Isomee said.

"She's dying. I broke her leg. She's old, so old and tired. She's been suffering from a broken heart for years."

The bird twitched and her eyes flickered open. Her breathing became deeper.

"What's she doing?" Isomee asked.

"I think she's smelling me."

"Why would she do that?" Isomee asked, stroking the chostri's neck.

A smile broke across Brackenbelly's face.

"Actually, she's smelling the scent that's on me. I need to go back to the surface and get Bramble. Will you stay here?"

"Of course," Isomee said, sitting on the floor next to the chostri. "Why do we need Bramble?" Isomee asked, though she was certain she already knew the answer.

"We're going to help right a wrong."

"Yes," Isomee said, finally knowing that what she had guessed *was* the truth. "I think we should."

"I'll try not to be too long," Brackenbelly said, carefully handing the bird over to her. Then he was off.

Isomee looked down into the chostri's sad eyes. Her family had brought this poor bird all this pain.

"I'm sorry," she said.

The chostri blinked and let out a small, strangled cry.

"My great-great-great-grandfather stole your eggs, didn't he?"

The chostri just lay there. Isomee didn't know if she could understand her words, but she hoped the old chostri would at least see and hear that she was sorry.

"Am I too late?" Brackenbelly called out a few minutes later as he rushed back into the cave, Bramble at his side.

"You're just in time, I think," Isomee said sadly.

Brackenbelly brought Bramble closer and she sat on the floor next to the old chostri, tucking her legs under her body.

"Come on," Brackenbelly whispered.

The feral chostri lifted her head from Isomee's legs and weakly turned her long neck towards Bramble.

The two birds looked at each other for a few moments and then began squawking as they gently rubbed their cheeks against each other. Soon the two chostri began to make contented sounds like a cat's purr.

"This is Bramble's mother, isn't it?" Isomee said, pointing at the injured chostri.

The uma nodded.

"Remember how your uncle told me Bramble was one hundred? One of the original eggs that hatched?" Brackenbelly stopped talking for a moment and stroked the dying chostri's head. "She can rest now. One hundred years was a terrible price to pay for one hundred paces, but at least at the end, she's got to see one of her precious babies."

The old chostri lowered her head once more and looked at Bramble, her long lost child.

Isomee started to cry again, but she was certain she saw happiness in the old chostri's eyes as they slowly flickered shut.

Twenty-Six

The walk back to Hogg-Bottom farm was sad and quiet.

After the old chostri had died, Brackenbelly sent Isomee and Bramble outside. She'd done as she was told. She hadn't done it because she was supposed to, like when her uncle told her to do things, but because she knew why. Brackenbelly wanted to bury the old chostri and spare her and Bramble any more pain.

The sun was up by the time they left the abandoned farm and Isomee wondered what her uncle would be doing.

Nothing, probably.

Would he be worried about their whereabouts? Or would he be more worried about his lack of breakfast?

Isomee wanted to speak to Brackenbelly about a thousand and one different things that were whizzing around in her head but wasn't sure what to say.

Finally, Hogg-Bottom farm appeared on the horizon and Brackenbelly broke the silence.

"I take it you haven't seen that farm before?"

"No, Uncle doesn't let me travel very far," she answered.

"I think it belonged to your family once. Your uncle said the Hogg-Bottoms moved on and built better houses. I think that place was one of those houses and Bramble's mother somehow managed to trace her eggs there. By the time she found it, though, your family had moved and she didn't know where to go next. Somehow she found her way to your present barn."

"She had a long time to look," Isomee said.

"Yes, she did," Brackenbelly replied, sadly.

"Why did she take me?"

"Chostri have a really strong sense of smell. I think she may have recognised your scent from the relative who stole her eggs."

"So she wanted revenge?"

"Maybe," Brackenbelly said. "I'd like to think she hoped you would feel sorry for her and give her babies back."

"I was going to, but she attacked me before I had the chance."

Isomee looked at her friend and it suddenly dawned on her. Now he'd solved the mystery, Brackenbelly would take Bramble and leave. Isomee walked onto the field of Hogg-Bottom farm in silence.

"I'm going to take Bramble back to the barn. I made her a promise," Brackenbelly said.

"What promise was that?"

"I told her it was up to her if she came with me."

"If she says no, will you stay here?"

Isomee didn't know if uma facial expressions were the same as humans', but the look on his face told her all she needed to know.

"I can't stay here, Isomee. I like to keep moving. I like to explore the world. See new things."

"Can't I come with you? You said I should leave here."

Brackenbelly put his hand on her shoulder. He looked her in the eyes and shook his head.

Isomee opened her mouth to speak but he walked off with Bramble before she could say a word.

A tear slipped from Isomee's eye and she turned to look at the house. She wanted to call it her home but it wasn't. It was just a place where she slept and worked.

Isomee looked back at the barn. Brackenbelly had disappeared inside and soon he would be gone forever.

In one day she had learned so many things. Could she go back to living the life of a slave?

Brackenbelly had shown her that the life she led was wrong. There was a better life. She just had to take it.

Isomee stood up straight and walked towards the house. She opened the front door, took a deep breath, wished herself luck and stepped into the kitchen. It was cold. Because she hadn't been there, the fire had gone out.

Uncle Hogg-Bottom was sat at the table.

"The fire's out. The animals haven't been fed. And... neither... have... I."

"Uncle, I can explain," she began and then stopped herself. She could hear how weak she sounded. Already she was behaving like his little slave.

"While you've been out playing with your freaky little friend I've—"

The front door opened and Brackenbelly stepped inside. He walked to the wobbly table and put a pouch on it.

"Have you even asked Isomee where she's been?" he said.

"N... no," Hogg-Bottom stammered.

"Then perhaps you should," Brackenbelly said. "Your problem's been solved. You'll find your money in that pouch. It's occurred to me that you might've already known what it was out there. I hope you didn't. "

"No, I didn't, I swear," gulped the fat, ugly man.

Isomee stood and watched as Brackenbelly studied her uncle. She was thinking the same thing he was. Her uncle was lying. He did know. She was sure.

"Don't be surprised if Isomee asks you some difficult questions. I'm taking Bramble and going."

Isomee watched as Brackenbelly walked back to the door. She wanted to go with him, but he was right. His life was dangerous. Besides, as she had told him yesterday, she couldn't leave. The farm was hers.

"Goodbye, Isomee," he said, "and remember what I said to you. I'm only sorry I can't take you with me."

Isomee felt tears filling the corner of her eyes but she wasn't going to cry, not in front of her uncle.

Brackenbelly reached behind him and placed a canvas bundle into her hands. Then he turned and walked out of the kitchen without looking back.

Isomee watched the front door close and then glanced across at Hogg-Bottom.

"We'll talk later," he said, and got up and left.

Isomee sat down at the table and opened the bundle. It was the bolas. She held it in her hands, remembering the last twenty-four hours. She looked at the stones and thought of her mother. What would she have wanted for her daughter? The memory of Bramble and her mother rubbing each other's faces flashed through Isomee's mind.

Families loved each other. Cared for each other. Encouraged each other. Isomee looked at her uncle's bedroom door. He did none of these things. But she didn't have to be like him.

Isomee hurriedly stuffed the weapon back into the canvas bag, and with it tucked under one arm, ran to her bedroom and grabbed something off the back of her door.

She turned and ran back out of her room. If she was quick, it wouldn't be too late.

"Wait!" Isomee called as she burst out of the house.

Brackenbelly was climbing onto Bramble's back.

"Isomee..." Brackenbelly started.

She shook her head.

"I wanted you to have this so you'll remember me." She held up the special halter she'd designed for Thorn. "It will help Bramble go faster when you're in danger. And you're hopeless at putting normal ones on."

Brackenbelly smiled.

"I will never forget you, I promise."

"And I will always remember you."

Isomee stepped back and watched Brackenbelly ride away until he slipped over the horizon.

"Isomee?" It was her uncle calling.

"I'm coming," she answered.

"No need to rush. Let's ride into town and get something nice to eat," he called back.

Isomee smiled. It sounded like he meant it. Maybe the beast of Hogg-Bottom farm had been tamed by the grey skinned stranger after all.

With one final wave to Brackenbelly, Isomee turned and walked back into the house she now hoped she could finally call a home.

The adventure continues

Coming soon!

Acknowledgements

This story wouldn't have been possible without the considerable help, support and advice from many people. Of those, I would like to send special thanks to Sally, Louise, Elene, Maria, but most of all, Nichola and William, my son.

About the Author

Gareth lives in a world of his own along with his family, superhero comics, books, films and computer games. He likes to deliberately say words wrong, plays the violin, the ukulele and Singstar.

Gareth is a Patron of Reading.

Also available from Amazon as paperbacks and Kindle eBook

Signed copies also available from

gareth-baker.com

To save the future he must become a hero from the past

TIME GUARDIANS
THE MINOTAUR'S ECLIPSE
Gareth Baker

A holiday to another country becomes a journey to another time and a fight against an ancient evil.

ROGUE RACER

GARETH BAKER

WHAT STARTS OFF AS A FUN
COMPUTER GAME, SOON
BECOMES SOMETHING FAR
MORE SERIOUS.

Coming Soon

New powers, new friends, new dangers

TIME GUARDIANS
THE CENTAUR'S CURSE
Gareth Baker

Find out more at

gareth-baker.com

Videos

Games

Activities

News

Sign up for the newsletter
and get all the latest news

Please try to find some time
to review this book on
Amazon.

Thank You.

35502899R00113

Printed in Poland
by Amazon Fulfillment
Poland Sp. z o.o., Wrocław